THE THINGS WE NEED

A NOVEL

ANTONIO ROBINSON

The Things We Need, a novel
Copyright © 2022 by Antonio Robinson

First Edition 2022

ISBN Paperback: 978-0-578-37712-4
ISBN Hardcover: 978-0-578-36906-8
ISBN Ebook: 978-0-578-29499-5
Library of Congress Control Number: 2022903233

Cover design by: Kristen Thorley
Edited by: Bass Jenkins

Antonio Robinson Publishing
Charlotte, NC 28217

PRINTED IN THE UNITED STATES OF AMERICA
1 2 3 4 5 6 7 8 9 0

"Crime is as much a condition as an intention."
-Lewis F. Korns

THE THINGS WE NEED

This is a true story. At the request of those still living, the names have been changed. Out of respect for the dead, the rest has been told exactly as it transpired.

CHAPTER 1

Life was rough and fast in the bad part of town.

On his hourly, this is where he was. Reggie Skinter. Early thirties and still no real idea where he was headed. He just knew that he'd need to make money to achieve some sort of freedom. But freedom aside, making a livable income would do.

Competitive Inn. The kind of motel police added to their daily route because of the murder, drugs, prostitution, and fights that festered in the area. Easy pickings for cops looking for low-hanging fruit.

They had the cheapest weekly price at $300 which is why Reggie settled on it. Not all motels offered weekly stays and the prices could hit $500 or better for the ones that did. Even the shitty motels were expensive. He'd lucked up as Competitive wasn't a chain and they didn't have to jack up their prices. Given the circumstances of life in the area, people would always need a place to stay for extended periods. He noticed the sanitation score on the wall in the lobby when he was paying for his first week's stay. It was a 78.6 which was a C in regards to the letter grade. Besides the fact that they had to keep the score in the open, it also gave them an out if anyone complained about how dirty and antique-looking the motel was. *This is what you signed up for* the score signified.

He'd been working at Fair Zone Carpet Cleaners for a year and moved in a couple of months after he'd started working.

The comforter had cigarette burns and there were bloodstains in the carpet that couldn't be washed out. Because blood doesn't wash out. But it lightened to the point where it almost blended into the multicolored, patterned carpet.

Reggie knew better though. Blood always looked like blood to him. And in this place, it was unquestionably spilled by the victim of some violent crime. Death may or may not have spared them.

The bed had no headboard and the lamps on the nightstands gave the room an ugly yellow-orangish color. The pictures that were hung were dollar store portraits of landscapes that didn't exist.

He wanted to rent an apartment but had been told by countless property managers that he didn't qualify because he didn't make enough to be considered a potential renter. They wanted triple the price of rent to move in. He neither understood nor liked this idea. As long as you could afford the rent and pay your bills, what difference did it make how much one made? To him, it was just another way to keep the have nots with less than they already needed. But he had no say so in the matter. Discouraged, he stopped looking after a while.

He was renting a room in the home of a Latino man by the name of Mateo before his stay at Competitive. Though he only lived in his home for a small amount of time, Reggie liked Mateo. They weren't friends but spoke often when neither were working. Mostly hanging out on the back patio drinking beers. Mateo kept food and alcohol in his home and threw a party every weekend. Women were in constant rotation. Reggie had crossed paths with a few half-dressed brown skinned Cuban women stumbling out of Mateo's room when he went to shower before work on some mornings. They'd smile and finish dressing before leaving. Reggie usually nodded and continued with his business. When Mateo's cousin came into town, he'd told Reggie he had two weeks to find a new place to live. Though he hadn't kicked him out, it felt like it. Reggie had been paying on a month-to-month basis so he didn't put up a fight. And even if he did, family always came first.

He'd rented several rooms before, but this instance had left him feeling desolate. He made up his mind then that he'd live on his own and moved into Competitive two weeks later. It wasn't supposed to be permanent, but then again, nothing ever is.

Competitive had a front and backside. The lobby was at the front. The rooms on this side were even numbers. The odd numbered rooms were at the back. Reggie was at the back in room 223. It was next to the last room. No elevator was necessary as there were only two floors. He did have a good view of the comings and goings at the motel. Alone and toking his blunt, he almost forgot about the problems that arose around him.

"Bitch! A nigga get out here every day trying to do for you and your fucking daughter!"

The couple next door, room 221, was going at it again. The walls were thin and their arguments were thunderous. They were living at Competitive before Reggie moved in and, for the most part, seemed to get along decently when they'd all first cross paths. But you never knew what was going on behind closed doors in other people's relationships. Not unless the walls were thin.

A roach crawled along the wall separating the two rooms. He'd grown used to the sight of the pest that nested in the motel. He could tell from the light brown coloring and dark parallel stripes on their back that they were German cockroaches. A smoky brown cockroach would pop up on occasion. Especially the day after heavy rain. But the majority were German. He remembered reading somewhere that roaches carried bacteria that caused asthma and a few other health-related issues. *How many people have died from staying here?* The thought crossed his mind often.

The mini-fridge was unplugged when he first moved in and roaches used the dark space for their nest. They froze once he plugged it back in again. He swept the frozen pests into a grocery bag and threw the bag in the big blue dumpster on the side of the building. He was a regular in the lobby the first two months of his stay. They called an exterminator after the last time he complained. The roaches were gone a week later, but one by one he started seeing them again.

He grabbed the can of Rid-A-Bug from atop the dresser and sprayed the roach that had now come to a halt on the wall. He watched as it tried to crawl through the thick puddle created from the spray. It slowed and eventually died. Reggie noted how spider like the roach looked with its legs sprawled out as it sank into eternity. *This is where things come to die* he thought absentmindedly.

He took another drag of his blunt and grabbed the $5 scratch-off he'd purchased across the street at Smiley's Mini Mart after work. He'd never won more than $50 on one of them but he played often. His eyes were on the jackpot and what it could do to help his current impoverished situation.

"Every fucking day for you and your daughter! How bout you call her sorry ass daddy and tell him to send her some money? Huh? You can't. Cause he don't give a fuck about y'all!"

Reggie knew the "her" Money was referring to was Deborah's fourteen-year-old daughter Victoria. He'd seen her face only a few times as she was either in the room or out with Deborah during the day. As unlikely as he knew it to be, he wished she was asleep during their sparring matches. The rent was due. Deborah launched a verbal assault whenever Money couldn't pay his half of the rent.

Money, like most people Reggie encountered, was just trying to get by.

This fight was only verbal. They'd turn physical on the occasion Deborah got sick of listening to Money's excuses. Legitimate or not.

"I'm the one taking penitentiary chances out here. And all I get in return is this bullshit!? I'm gettin' bout sick o' yo ass," Money said.

Reggie finished scratching his ticket. It was a bust. "Dammit," he said aloud.

He'd prefer to break even than to lose altogether, but he understood the odds. He'd tell himself that he wouldn't play again after he surmounted so many losses in a row. But he never stopped. In his mind, the possibility of winning outweighed the downside of losing. The downside was him going broke in the process. But life was a gamble. Scratching numbers on a ticket seemed like the safest bet.

He went over all the numbers meticulously and, seeing that he hadn't won, threw the ticket in the trash can next to the dresser.

"We need more money or we gon' be out on the street with the rest of those crackheads wandering around the city. I'm not built to live like that. I can't have my daughter out here like that," Deborah said.

"Listen, baby, I hear ya. I ain't gonna have y'all sleeping under some bridge or no shit like that. I'm gonna get more money coming in soon," Money said.

Reggie took a drag from his blunt and turned up the volume on the television. Another Law & Order rerun. He'd seen them all, but anything beat listening to tonight's episode of Stepfamily Feud. He cranked the volume until Detective Benson's voice drowned out the game show next door, took another hit of his blunt, and laid back on the bed. He blew smoke rings to the ceiling as the bud made his thoughts wander.

❄ ❄ ❄

"Man, I don't know what I'mma do wit her Reg."

The parking lot at the motel was full. That was normal for the weekend. It was empty during the week. That's where you saw who the regulars were. Reggie zipped up his gray hoodie and tucked his head as the night air blew through. Money tucked his head as well.

"It done got cold as hell early this year," Money said.

"It damn sure did," Reggie said.

Money passed the blunt to Reggie and lit a cigarette.

"All she do is ride my back. I know you heard us in there earlier."

Reggie was hoping Money wouldn't come back to the topic. He didn't care to talk about other people's relationships. Leave or don't was his advice if you wanted to call it that. But Money was cool and he never skimped on the weed so he listened. Reggie was only outside because he'd woken up with cotton mouth and went to the vending machine for a Coke. Money was standing outside smoking by the time he'd gotten back to his door.

"I can't make these fiends shop no faster. I'm pumping this shit on that god damn bike in there bout fast as I can," Money said pointing to his room door.

The bike he was referring to was a gray Schwinn mountain bike. Reggie didn't know how old the bike was, but it was still in good condition.

"If she pulled her weight maybe I could hold on to some extra change and get a car or something. Start making real sales," Money said and took a drag of his cigarette after.

Reggie pulled from the blunt and passed it back to Money.

"But anyway," Money said and took a hit from the blunt after. "I'm not finna talk yo' head off about that. She either gon' get over it or leave."

Money smoked in silence. Reggie stared at the license plate of a scooter parked in a parking spot below where the two were standing.

PRAZDALE-RAZEHELL it read.

Buzzed from the weed, it took Reggie a moment to figure out what it meant.

Praise Dale-Raise Hell it suddenly clicked in his head. It was original at least.

"They still hiring down at your job?"

The question broke through the silence. Reggie snapped out of his daze and looked over at Money who was studying the same license plate.

"Yeah, they hiring. You gotta fill out the application online," Reggie said.

"Man, I told you I don't do all that computer shit. I gotta go to the library and do all that...," Money drifted off and made a face. "Man. I told you all you gotta do is put in a good word for me. You already on the inside," Money said.

"Put in an application," Reggie repeated.

Money got silent again. He wasn't going to put in an application. He and Reggie knew it. He wouldn't say it out loud, but Reggie had a feeling Money never really learned how to use a computer. Or at least how to navigate the internet enough to put in applications. Which was a problem in present times because most, if not all, job applications needed to be filled out online. He couldn't remember the last time he'd walked in and asked whether or not a place was hiring. Everything was posted on job boards. That meant certain doom for Money and men like him. You either moved with the times or got steamrolled by them.

Praise Dale-Raise Hell

He looked back down at the license plate.

"One of y'all boys got toothpaste?"

The voice came from a man approaching in a red hoodie and blue jeans.

"What?" Money said.

"Toothpaste. Either one of you got any?" The man asked again.

Reggie and Money looked at each other confused. The man in the hoodie kept approaching.

"I got this chick in the room, but her breath stink. I can't let her put her mouth on me smelling like that," the man said stopping short of the two men.

He was holding one of those cheap toothbrushes that came in packs of five.

"I just need a little bit if one of y'all got some," he said.

Reggie got a kick out of the man's story. He turned to get his tube of toothpaste from his room. Money and the man stood in silence waiting for him to return. Money took the last drag of his cigarette and plucked it over the railing.

Sparks flickered across the pavement below when it landed.

Reggie returned and handed the toothpaste to the man. He squeezed some onto his brush and handed the tube back to Reggie.

"Good looking man," the man said and turned and left after.

Reggie and Money watched him until he reached his room.

"Messing with these dirty women that hang around here. Fuck toothpaste, he better have a condom," Money said.

Reggie laughed and nodded in agreement.

"But I'm bout to head back inside," Reggie said.

"Aight, big bruh. Don't forget about me down at that job," Money said.

Reggie decided not to repeat the obvious. He was high and ready to go back to sleep.

CHAPTER 2

"I'm gonna pluck ya belly button out ya navel! Every morning, you the loudest mutha-fucka in that goddamn shelter!"

The voice cut through the sounds of the drillers unearthing concrete as they worked to fix the streets in Uptown Charlotte. It was mid-October and the morning air was brisk as people scurried around one another focused only on their destinations.

Some of the mom-and-pop coffee shops and restaurants had ghosts, skeletons, and other Halloween related items on display in their windows.

Reggie had grown accustomed to these early morning standoffs between the homeless defunct roaming the streets. Little money always resulted in little patience. The shelter was within earshot of the city's business district. Seemed a cruel joke to cram the rich and poor so close together, but they learned to tolerate one another. Ignored each other really. Reggie started to think of these little spats as Vaudeville for the city's commuters. A little show before retreating into the safety of their office buildings.

Fair Zone cleaned the floors in the shelters three times a year. Reggie had been assigned to the cleaning crew the last time and asked one of the workers at the shelter the process. The men and women were kicked out at 7:30 each morning and allowed back in after 4 pm. Young or old, unless they had a job, they'd prowl the streets. Most wound up in parks, libraries, or coffee shops to sleep. When it rained, they'd cram together underneath whatever store awnings they could until the owners forced them to move on. A few ended up on side streets where they'd sleep in any doorway that had the least amount of foot traffic.

Though he had seen a handful of Whites and Mexicans come from the shelter, they were Black men and women for the most part.

The man yelling the insults had spotted his target across the street; a twenty-something, average height, overweight dreadhead. The man himself was tall and thick around the waist in the way weight settles as age creeps on. His accent, just as thick, was that of a northerner. The new wave of people moving to the south had created an odd mixture of hospitable practices.

13

"You got one more time to fuck my sleep up boy! ONE. MORE. TIME!" The older man shouted across the street.

By this point, the business crowd making their way to work and students heading for the Lynx had taken notice. They didn't stop to watch, but their strides became noticeably slower as they focused on what was unfolding on this cool fall morning.

"Sure bitch," said the dreadhead.

"You on the clock boy! And your time bout up!" The older gentleman yelled.

The dreadhead smirked and swaggered in the opposite direction. The older gentleman watched for a moment.

"Young mutha-fucka," he mumbled under his breath and turned and walked away after.

Reggie grabbed his chip bucket from inside of the baby blue 08' Chevy Express Cargo Van they'd assigned to him once he'd made crew chief six months ago. You had to lift on the door to close it because the hinge was off, the air conditioner was constantly going in and out, and it needed a front-end alignment. He didn't mind any of that though. Reggie couldn't afford a car so work was the only time he drove. Clunker or not, he enjoyed getting behind the wheel.

Fair Zone was printed on both sides of the van in black. There was a yellow lightning bolt between Fair

Zone. The two official colors for the company were baby blue and yellow.

The uniform consisted of black Dickie pants and a baby blue shirt with a smaller version of the logo printed on the front. They were also required to wear steel-toe black boots. A new pair was given to each cleaner once they'd officially been hired on.

The assistant he'd been paired with for the day had called out. Dustin Gardner. A young White boy. He was new to the company and Reggie hadn't worked with him yet. He seemed cool from what he'd gathered in passing conversation. Not much education and eager to make a buck.

He grabbed his tablet and walked to the second floor of the apartment complex.

Mary Warren was the woman's name whose living room Reggie now stood. Middle-aged White lady. Short and slim, she wore black, square glasses and had a friendly smile. Her hair was salt and pepper and she wore it in a bob cut. No doubt trying to look younger. Recently widowed she'd decided it best to downsize since the kids had long moved out. Her husband, Wes Warren, had been a firefighter in the city. His station got called in for a house fire. The house was ablaze when they arrived, but they went inside to search for any casualties. The roof collapsed not long after they entered the home. Five in total died that day. Wes was among the dead.

15

The apartment was well kept. There was a large sectional in the center of the living room with end tables on both sides. Lamps and family pictures sat atop both. Nothing too expensive. Reggie had gotten in the habit of taking inventory of every home, apartment, and condominium he cleaned. Mainly because it was stressed not to break people's things while they were in their living space. Fair Zone would replace the broken item, but they'd also take the money out of the worker's check.

"Would you like for me to clean the open areas or move some of this furniture around and clean underneath them?" Reggie asked while taking inventory of the room.

He asked this question only when he was working solo. He could get his assistant to do the heavy lifting otherwise, but that was a tall task to handle alone.

"The sofa's kinda heavy so don't worry about it. Just those two end tables in here. And be sure to get underneath the bed in my room," she said empathizing with the job in front of him.

"My wand will go about two feet under the bed. Company policy we don't move beds and electronics."

"That's fine," she said and smiled after. "I didn't expect you to move the whole damn bed by yourself," she said laughing at her own humor.

"Thank you," he said and smiled back.

After getting her to sign the "Slip & Fall" notice, a document that alerted the customer that the carpet would be wet and to watch their step when stepping from wet carpet to hard surfaces that basically absolved the company of any injury claims, Reggie left to set up the van.

❋ ❋ ❋

The job didn't take long. Setting up the van was the only heavy lifting he'd had to do. Mary watched t.v. in the living room the entire time Reggie cleaned and only got up when Reggie asked her to inspect the rooms. Getting the customer to inspect the rooms before closing out helped to minimize redo cleanings. They'd still find things to complain about sometimes but if the customer felt something was missed or not cleaned to their liking, this step helped to straighten things out while the cleaners were still in the home. They weren't paid for redo cleanings so it was sensible to get things right the first time.

She tipped him $20 when he finished and offered him a cup of water. He took it to be polite but poured it out as soon as he drove off. He didn't drink tap water from people's homes or in general.

Tips were always welcome. Reggie needed the extra money. The most Reggie'd received in tips in one day was $100. He bought a twelve-pack of Budweiser and ate crab legs that day.

❋ ❋ ❋

"I'm not very good at keeping up with a home."

Reggie smiled at the pretty young woman he was now staring at. Looking around her apartment, she was right. There were clothes tossed in various corners of the living room and even a couple of shirts slung over the back of the couch. He could see a few dishes in the sink and overall clutter in the room. But there wasn't a smell and her apartment was mostly cluttered as opposed to being dirty. Reggie had been in enough houses and apartments to tell the difference.

"Don't even worry about it," he said.

Her name was Arrika Smith from what he'd seen in the notes. She was a new customer for the company so he was the first to be cleaning her carpets. She looked to be in her mid-twenties. A young professional woman.

"Yeah, I work in sales. I try to keep up with this place, but I'm so tired when I get home. I'll pick up or move anything you need me to," Arrika said looking around the apartment.

"Ummm. That's not necessary. I can move all of this stuff myself. There's nothing heavy in here. You can move your clothes out the way though," he said not wanting to touch her laundry.

Arrika moved with a jump. "Right," she said.

Reggie watched her pick her clothes up and sling them across her forearm. She was pretty, but he didn't care much for younger women.

"Okay. Just get in here, in the bedroom, and steam vac the closet in the bedroom too. There shouldn't be any major stains or anything. Just needs a good cleaning," Arrika said.

"I'll knock it out for you," Reggie said.

"Thank you. I'll be in the kitchen on my laptop if you need anything," she said.

Reggie nodded and went into the bedroom where he'd already set up his wand.

❄ ❄ ❄

"Onions and cilantro?"

The voice belonged to the Mexican lady who owned the food truck in front of Competitive. It was painted red, but the red had faded and gotten a dusty look over the years. It had no name, but it said *TACOS* in large letters next to the window where you placed your order. There was a Mexican smiling in one of those Speedy Gonzales hats with a pointed mustache holding a tray of food painted on the truck as well. When anyone other than a Mexican came to the window, she only asked for payment and what you wanted to order in English. Reggie had made the mistake of asking about the menu when he first came to the stand. She fumbled over what to say until Reggie eventually settled on a steak taco. It said *Carne Asada* on the menu outside of the truck, but he'd heard the Mexican lady refer to it as steak when she spoke to an English-speaking customer so he kept it simple. He'd watch what other Mexicans ordered and pointed at the item while she was making it when he wanted something different. The Cuban Sandwich was good, but he'd gotten her to take the pineapples off after the first time. Pineapples on food was a sin as far as he was concerned. Her voice was heavy but feminine, and she was a damn good cook. Made the best steak tacos on this side of town. The long lines at lunchtime backed Reggie's idea of this.

"Yes, with the green sauce please," he responded.

She nodded and threw some oil over the steak on the grill causing it to sizzle. She chopped the meat and flipped it with two steel spatulas.

A car pulled up behind him. He turned and saw a lone Mexican man looking at the food truck from his window. It was a beat-up black Toyota Camry. Either a 92' or 93' model from the build. Reggie could tell he was pondering whether he wanted food from the truck or not. He pulled in a moment later and got out of his car.

The Mexican woman stepped away from the grill to take his order. Reggie watched as they conversed in Spanish. The woman jotted his order down on a yellow legal pad.

She confirmed his order and said, "Diez minutos," before turning and putting more steak onto the grill. Reggie knew this meant ten minutes in Spanish from hearing it so many times.

She threw a tortilla on the grill and flipped it after a minute and waited for the opposite side to heat through.

Reggie looked towards the motel. The parking lot was sparse. Besides a few cars, he spotted a white pick-up truck with a trailer attached near the back of the motel. There was a Mexican man in an orange sweatshirt sitting at the top of the steps leading to the second floor. Reggie knew he was a construction worker. The orange sweatshirt was a dead giveaway. He saw them constantly when he had to drive into Uptown for a job. They were either working on the streets or on one of what seemed like thousands of new housing and apartment developments. Charlotte was making leaps and bounds to house all of the young professionals migrating to her city, but little for the local residents or those already waist-deep in debt. New people brought new prices which always led to new problems. Or old problems that just never got fixed.

He heard the Mexican woman wrapping up his taco and turned to face the window. She threw the taco now wrapped in aluminum foil into a white paper bag. She tossed a tiny packet of salt, a cup of Verde sauce, a lime, and a napkin into the bag and folded the top.

"$3.50," she said smiling but still holding the bag.

Reggie handed her $4 and waved her off for the change.

She looked to be over forty. Her youth was in her eyes. Pretty no doubt. Like most Mexican women, she was short. The fact that her tacos tasted so good always made him think about trying to bone her. But he didn't speak Spanish and most Mexican women, especially in poorer areas, stuck to their own. And even if they didn't,

21

they rarely showed interest in Black men outside of lustful intentions. He'd never slept with a Spanish speaking woman before. There was a maid that was working at the motel that he thought hit on him once, but he didn't pursue it. He only saw her on weekends as he was at work during their normal cleaning hours, but she lingered at his room whenever she knew he was in. On one occasion, she pulled out her phone and showed him a picture of herself in a dress. From the looks, she'd gone out to a club. She pointed to the picture and then back at herself. He got the idea she was trying to show him how well she cleaned up. She was attractive, but not his type overall. He smiled and pretended he didn't understand. The language barrier seemed like too much of a hassle if all he was looking for was to get laid. He didn't see her the next weekend or any other weekends after.

He checked his bag and left.

CHAPTER 3

It was the weekend. Although it was mandatory for all employees of Fair Zone to be available on weekends, he rarely got called in. He spent weekends drinking, getting stoned, binging shows, or watching ESPN. He spoke with Money from time to time but avoided him otherwise. Money tended to beg him for a job at Fair Zone. Reggie didn't handle hiring and couldn't be bothered to vouch for anyone. Especially a known drug dealer (cause Money sold coke and pills on top of weed) with a volatile attitude. When things went left, the managers would be looking at him. Reggie had enough issues to deal with and couldn't be bothered with taking on the burdens of another man.

There wasn't much to do otherwise. He'd find his way to a bar in Uptown on the rare occasion, but he didn't like the crowd. There were way too many people repping their side which usually led to a fight breaking out. He'd had a bottle pulled on him by some drunk local kid during the summer. Understanding that he was drunk, Reggie didn't entertain the threat. Two of the guys' friends came and pulled him back.

"You always do this shit bruh," Reggie heard one of them say as they tugged him in the opposite direction.

No crowd had gathered and, from what Reggie could tell, no one was even paying them any mind. The two left with their friend and that was it. Violence in the city seemed volatile, unnecessary, and trivial.

That had been the last time he ventured into the city for the nightlife. He didn't mind a good fight, but the younger generation skipped their fisticuffs lessons. They were killers. And as much as one wanted to stay alive, death doesn't care about a name.

And besides, the current state of the world was untrusting. With all of the mass shootings and general unrest in the public, Reggie felt it wise to stick to himself. He had enough on his plate as it was. Some unstable sociopath taking out his rage in public because he never got laid in high school was far down his list of things to fall victim to.

There was a knock on the door.

Reggie wasn't expecting company. Besides that, no one he knew lived in the city so he didn't hang out with anybody he considered a friend. He heard laughter and little feet running down the stairs.

He got up and looked out of the window in time to catch the heads of a Mexican boy and a Black boy as they hopped down the last two steps.

He'd seen them hanging out and knew that they'd made a game of knocking on residents' doors and taking off running. It was annoying depending on how frequently they knocked on his door in a day, but it didn't bother him. They were just kids and, given the kind of trouble they could be getting into, this was just harmless fun.

Reggie closed the curtain and walked back to the bed.

Boom!

The knock was more pronounced this time. Reggie even jumped a little. He turned and rushed to the door. This time he'd let them know to cu-

"Bring back my fucking kids!"

Reggie froze before opening the door and looked around the room. He had no children of his own and didn't know of any that may be hiding in his room.

The voice belonged to a female.

There was a loud bang on his window as she repeated herself and then it stopped.

Reggie opened his door and looked down the row of rooms.

A skinny Black woman was hollering in to her phone banging on doors and windows as she spoke.

Reggie guessed she was speaking to the father of
her children. Custody wars were the norm on this side of
town. He watched as she walked past the rooms. Heads
poked out of occupied rooms to see what was happening.

No one said anything to her though. They knew
she'd only channel her anger towards them. No need to
waste a Saturday on matters that had nothing to do with
you.

She made it to the end and headed down the
steps.

One by one, everyone poked their heads back into
their rooms and closed their door. Reggie did the same.

❄ ❄ ❄

He had $50 to his name and it would have to last until
payday on Friday. It'd be $30 for the week in another
moment. He knew he'd be buying a couple of scratch-
offs to try and supplement his income. Winning an extra
$100 would help to keep him fed until he got paid at the
end of the week.

He stood in the QT staring at the lottery vending
machine. He normally avoided the vending machine
lottery tickets because it didn't feel as authentic as an
actual person handing you a ticket, but it did give him
time to study the tickets because there was never a line at
the ticket machine.

He'd been a gambler since he was young. They
gambled on everything growing up in his neighborhood.
Basketball games in the street, cards, video games;

anything that helped to take money out of someone's pocket and put it into your own. The habit had turned to lotto tickets after he graduated high school and had been on his own for a few years. The odds were less in his favor and he had no control over who won, but the chance of hitting big had found its way into his subconscious.

He made up his mind to spend $15 on tickets. After he left the gas station, he'd head over to the Family Dollar and grab some cheap lunch meat, bread, and a case of water. Sandwiches would have to do for the next couple of days.

A Black woman who looked to be in her mid-twenties was making a hot dog. She and Reggie locked eyes momentarily. She smiled and Reggie smiled back. She glanced at the lottery machine and then back at Reggie. Her lips curved into a frown. Reggie noticed, turned back to the machine, and continued studying the tickets.

He knew she was judging him for playing scratch-offs, but it didn't bother him. As soon as they walked out of the station, they'd be two more faces in the crowd. And this encounter would be forgotten.

None of the tickets stood out. Instinctually, this bothered him because part of gambling was instincts. You went with what stood out. He continued scanning the tickets.

27

A man with salt and pepper hair walked in and stood behind him. At first glance, he reminded Reggie of Anthony Hopkins. They nodded at one another in acknowledgment and Reggie turned back to the machine. He was now consciously aware that he needed to make his decision in haste.

He settled on 2 $5 tickets, 2 $2 tickets, and 1 $1 ticket. He waited for the tickets to dispense, grabbed them, and left the gas station.

❄ ❄ ❄

Finished eating his two sandwiches, Reggie stared at the lottery tickets on the bed. He'd placed them next to one another and studied them. He knew about the *White Line Theory* and had found that it was true most of the time. The theory being that tickets with the white line across the top or the bottom of the ticket were guaranteed winners. Reggie had won on most of his tickets with the line but had broken even on the tickets more often than not.

The only ticket with the white line was one of the $2 tickets. He set it to the side and scratched the remainders. He lost on all but one of those tickets. He broke even on one of the $5 tickets. He scratched the $2 ticket with the white line. He symbol hunted first. This was the process of scratching the numbers first to try and find one of the winning symbols that all lottery tickets had. He found a 2x symbol. Aware of the fake multipliers that NC Lottery used(fake because rarely were the winnings more than double the value of the ticket), he figured he won $4. His thoughts were confirmed when he scratched the spot and revealed the $2 underneath. He scratched the winning numbers and saw the symbol was his only win. $9 in total. Minus the food, he had a little under $40 for the week. He threw the losers in the trash and set the two winning tickets beside the television.

❄ ❄ ❄

"Have you been here before?"

The chubby young Mexican employee at *Stick-Up Pawn Shop* (named this because the prices they offered on any item was robbery no doubt) asked Reggie.

He was used to hocking his stuff. He'd sold televisions, phones, and even laptops. When times had gotten tough, he wasn't able to eat any of that stuff so he'd sold it. Some of it he bought back when he was able to afford to, but he let the pawnshops keep most of the stuff he pawned. And by keep, meaning he didn't go back for it. He stopped gaining an attachment for things when he saw how quickly he'd had to get rid of them. Most of what he bought consisted of things he needed daily. He couldn't remember the last time he'd made a purchase just to have something or simply because he wanted it. Everything had to serve a purpose. Otherwise, it was just stuff. And that stuff usually ended up in places like this.

Today he was pawning a power drill he'd gotten from a customer at Fair Zone. The guy had been telling

Reggie about renovations he was thinking about making in his kitchen and wanted a little insight from a technician's standpoint on what he thought. Mostly questions about tile and grout vs hardwood. Reggie didn't know much beyond what he'd learned on the job but had given his opinion and gotten on with the job of cleaning his carpeted upstairs. The guy tipped Reggie $20 and gave him one of his old drills. Said he wasn't using it and was probably going to be selling it soon anyway. Reggie took it and thanked him, but had kept it in the room ever since.

Today was the first day it would come in handy.

"Yes, I've been here before," Reggie said.

It'd been a while since he'd pawned anything and they, like a lot of jobs, were a revolving door for employment. It'd been a new employee every time he pawned something. That made bargaining hard because if they knew you, they'd be more likely to work with you on what they could offer on the sale or pawn of whatever you were trying to hock.

"How much you looking to get?" The young employee asked.

Reggie hadn't looked up the value for the drill but had eyeballed a few that they had on the shelf. The larger ones were pricier, but the drills that were the closest in size to his were selling for $89 on average.

"Fifty dollars," Reggie said.

30

The employee reinspected the drill and looked it up on his computer.

He knew they were going to lowball him. Just how much was the question. But it was free money nonetheless. The money he had left from the tickets was about spent so this little boost would have to do for the moment. Two days into the workweek and he hadn't gotten any tips.

There were a couple of people in line behind him. They gazed around the shop at different items as they waited their turn. The guy behind Reggie was standing next to a 55-inch television. The kid behind him had an Xbox, controller, and a few games in hand. More stuff.

"I can do $30," the young employee said.

Reggie turned his attention back to the Stick-Up employee.

He had expected at least $40 but hadn't gotten his hopes up. He'd negotiated at this pawn shop before but wasn't really in the mood. But-

"You can't do $40?" Reggie said.

The employee looked at him and then back at the screen. He inspected the drill once more. Reggie knew this meant he was at least considering offering more. At the very least he'd say no and that would be that. No harm.

"I'll do $35 but that's as much as I can give you," the young employee said.

"That works for me," Reggie said.

The sale was finalized and Reggie left the pawnshop. The guy behind him slid his television up to the counter. As he exited, he heard the young Mexican ask the same question he was trained to ask every face that stepped in front of the counter.

"Have you been here before?"

CHAPTER 4

The crew chief and assistant got a percentage of all add-ons for their daily route, but the percentages were so low that it wasn't worth the hassle to make the sale. The way he and other employees reconciled this was to find a balance between side jobs and what they'd punch into the tablet. They preached commission but outside of the senior techs, no one ever hit commission. And the hourly was shit. $12. They set the hourly this low to encourage sales. Chris Patterson, the manager at Fair Zone, stressed that at the end of the day that's what the job was about. Selling. The only issue with that is that everybody didn't want to be sold to. They wanted the job they paid for and nothing more. Understandable depending on their financial standing. In a way, side jobs helped to even the playing field for both the workers and the customers. They got the work they wanted done at a price that kept them out of the loan office, and the workers made a bit of extra pocket change to get them through the week. You'd be fired on the spot if you were caught doing a deal with the customer. Sure you could clean additional areas, but without putting it into your tablet, it was considered theft.

Reggie had been at Fair Zone for a year and had figured a way around getting caught, as most of the employees over time had learned to do. He went weeks at a time sometimes without doing side jobs. It all depended on what the customers needed on the day of their appointment.

Another solo day. Reggie checked the tablet once he pulled into Parkwood Apartments. He liked to know customers cleaning history. Although he had never cleaned the apartment, the history showed they'd been there three times previously. He checked to see if there were any notes on the job. Nothing.

He had gotten deodorizer each time so Reggie expected to be greeted by a pet. The apartment was on the second floor. He unplugged the tablet from the cigarette lighter, gathered himself, and went up.

❄ ❄ ❄

Reggie stood at the door in the breezeway. There was no one else on the floor except for him. He knocked and, to his surprise, didn't hear a dog rushing to the door barking as though it had been starved to the point of being rabid.

Must have a cat Reggie thought to himself.

34

Customers without pets rarely got deodorizer. Frankly, barring extreme circumstances, it was unnecessary. He'd been in enough affluent neighborhoods to know that most people who lived in these areas had pets. It was the new status symbol for upper-middle-class America. Exotic things. To own some weird-looking animal because money bought anything within reason. And, with enough of it, one didn't need a reason at all.

The door opened and a cloud of smoke drifted out.

An older White gentleman answered. His white mustache was tinted yellow. Discolored from what was most likely years of smoking and his eyes looked a little wild to Reggie. He took note but brushed it off. He wasn't a psychologist. He was here to clean the carpet.

"Hiya?"

"How's it going? I'm Reggie," he said

"Hi, Reggie. Kenneth."

They shook and Kenneth stood at the door staring as if he didn't know why Reggie had shown up.

"Got some work for me today?" Reggie asked cutting through the awkward silence.

"Yeah," Kenneth responded sheepishly. "Had my grandson over yesterday and he got sick," he said looking down.

That's why I didn't hear any pets Reggie thought to himself. *And that's the reason he's getting deodorizer* he thought right after.

"Upset stomach. Shit everywhere. He had the runs all night," Kenneth said.

"Okay. I've seen almost everything working this job so I'm not bothered. I get things happen sometimes," Reggie said trying to reassure Kenneth.

"Ooo k," Kenneth responded, opening the door so Reggie could see into his apartment. He backed up and Reggie stepped inside.

The smell hit him first. Reggie found himself involuntarily holding his breath. Kenneth had probably been chain smoking to mask it, but it hadn't worked.

There were shit trails from the living room to the bathroom and from the bedroom to the bathroom. Reggie also spotted cigarette burns in different spots in the carpet.

Old Coors Light and Bud Light cans were stacked beside the couch in the living room, the countertops in the kitchen were cluttered with canned goods, and the apartment was in bad shape overall. Reggie could tell by the looks of things that he wasn't a hoarder. At least they had some form of sentimentality for the shit they collected. Kenneth either didn't care enough to clean up after himself or wasn't in a mental space to understand that his internal struggle was having real world effects.

Reggie found it odd that he hadn't seen any pictures of Kenneth's kids or his grandson. Family pictures usually stood out. He also wondered who would let their child stay here. Familial relations be damned.

"Hey, I'm sorry man. It was coming out all night. I did my best, but, you know, kids are unpredictable," Kenneth said looking embarrassed.

Reggie, becoming skeptical, nodded and checked the full extent of the damage. His head moved up and down in his attempt to assess the damage done to the apartment and also make sure he didn't step in any of the feces.

There was a framed American flag lying in the corner of the bedroom. The glass was dusty and a crack ran halfway down it. Military memorabilia were scattered throughout the room along with dirty clothes, old newspapers, magazines, and more empty beer cans. There was an old television sitting on top of the dresser in front of the bed. Clothes were sticking out of open drawers. Loose change sat beside the television. Reggie caught a glimpse of himself on the dusty screen. He saw Kenneth staring at him.

Kenneth was ex-military though now a shell of his former self. Reggie guessed army but didn't bother to ask. He had bumped into plenty of vets living on the streets. Like the rest, he didn't have his shit together, but Kenneth was one of the lucky ones that didn't have to beg for his daily bread.

And lucky for him. He'd seen homeless vets standing in the middle of traffic trying to get spare change. They didn't care about getting hit by oncoming cars. Just stood there. Waiting for spare change or someone to put them out of their misery.

He always felt a bit of pity for these individuals as it seemed they'd dedicated themselves to their country and got welcomed back a few marbles short to function in civilized society. The irony of not being able to cope in a country you were once willing to die for was not lost on him.

Sadly, Kenneth was one of the lucky ones.

Kenneth followed Reggie into the bedroom and began tossing newspapers and beer cans to one side of the room.

"You don't have to worry about cleaning the whole carpet," Kenneth said not looking at Reggie. "Just clean where the shit is. The carpet's fucked. I don't care much about the rest of it," he said emphasizing the spot where the damage was done.

"I have to be honest with you. I'll be able to get all of the ... shit(he didn't like cursing around the customers but it felt weird saying "poo" or "doo-doo") off of the carpet, but those stains are permanent most likely. They'll lighten, but won't disappear," Reggie said.

He was positive Kenneth didn't have a grandson or even a kid of his own for that matter. He was just too embarrassed to admit that as a grown man he had no control of his bowels. And maybe he didn't try to control them. Either way, Reggie played along with the ruse.

"I understand. I'm not asking for no miracle or nothing like that. Just do the best you can" he said pausing as if he were reading Reggie's thoughts. "Thanks, man," Kenneth said.

❄ ❄ ❄

Reggie managed to avoid stepping in shit during the walkthrough but made sure to put on shoe covers before re-entering the apartment.

The feces cleaned up as he'd expected, but the stains that were left behind suggested that this was a pattern for Kenneth.

Why didn't they mention his antics in the customer notes? Reggie thought to himself as he cleaned. It would have been simple to give the next cleaner a heads up. Chris should have at least mentioned something before he left the Route Room this morning. This must be a rite of passage. He decided not to make a note either. *Good luck* he thought.

He hadn't opted to get the tile in his bathroom cleaned. The trail into the bathroom was so bad if he'd closed the door, he would have slid shit back onto the carpet.

He sprayed the deodorizer in the bedroom first and made his way out to the living room. The deodorizer helped to mask the smell, but Reggie knew it'd return within a few hours. Nothing short of replacing the carpets would get that smell permanently out of the apartment.

39

Kenneth was sitting on the couch in the living room, and, like most customers, he watched Reggie the entire time. Puffing away on his cigarette as he did so. The television was on one of those afternoon court shows.

Reggie sprayed the carpet next to the television stand and turned back in the direction of Kenneth who by this point had stood up and was pissing into a jug sitting on the coffee table.

"Hey, I'm sorry man," Kenneth said and finished peeing.

Reggie didn't care for the apology. A combination of the set-in shit stains and this pissing incident confirmed Kenneth was the "grandson" who shit everywhere. Even worse, he wasn't sick when he did it. God Bless America.

Reggie quit spraying and left. He always packed up the van before spraying Scotchgard or deodorizer. He was grateful for this now. He heard the judge bang the gavel on the t.v. as he left.

❄ ❄ ❄

Cleaning human feces wasn't the norm for the job, but mental illness be damned, a man could only accommodate an affliction so much. And was pissing into a jug considered an affliction? Maybe not, but common human decency said he could have at least waited until Reggie was gone.

He called Chris on his way back to the station to explain why he hadn't collected payment. He laughed but was understanding. Chris agreed to call Kenneth and collect payment over the phone.

"Yeah. I was hoping he wouldn't come unwound while you were there," Chris said.

"Pulling his dick out while I'm in the house isn't unwound. He's fucking nuts, Chris. Someone should have told me about him," Reggie said.

He said a few more things to Chris, but his complaints fell on deaf ears. He could tell this was a normal conversation for the cleaners assigned to Kenneth's apartment and Chris couldn't be bothered with listening to any of it. He hung up the phone while Chris was making his speech about the importance of being a professional while on site.

Before he got out of the neighborhood, he pulled over and sprayed himself with the remaining deodorizer in the jug to try and kill the smell that was stuck in his nose. People in cars stared as they drove by.

❅ ❅ ❅

It was after 5 pm when he arrived back at the shop and most of the workers had left for the day. Reggie finished the nightly task of cleaning and parking the van and headed inside to the Route Room to hand in his tablet and gas card.

"Fuck y'all," Reggie said as he walked into the room.

Henry Baker, a Senior Carpet Tech at the company, and Chris were sitting in front of the computer

41

used to assign the daily routes. A couple of the workers who had probably stuck around to laugh at Reggie were conversing when he entered.

"You straight Reg?" Larry asked holding back his laugh.

Larry Stephenson was no older than 27. He'd been employed at Fair Zone a year when Reggie started. Easy going, but that was because he kept a vape pen filled with weed oil that'd he'd toke constantly throughout the day.

When Reggie first met Larry, he just figured he moved at his own pace. After being his assistant for a day, he realized that he was high most of the time. He wasn't a great cleaner, but he was fast and didn't get many complaints from customers. Reggie got the feeling Chris overlooked the fact that he smoked on company time because of this. Reggie never smoked at work and had turned down Larry's invitation on more than one occasion. The younger workers teased him about it, but it was just the way he was.

Reggie flipped Larry the bird.

The room lit up with laughter as they looked at Reggie. Larry even chuckled at the gesture. He shrugged and sat down on one of the desks in the room.

"I don't make the routes," Larry said not holding his laughter.

"Y'all set me up," Reggie said.

Chris came over and clapped Reggie's shoulders.

"Relax Reggie. He's harmless. Stuff like that happens to all of us here at some point," he said as he finished laughing.

The thought of a man who was ex-military being "harmless" didn't sit well with Reggie. Kenneth was anything but harmless. He was an old forgotten land mine waiting to be triggered.

"Damn right it does," Henry responded still sitting down. "This job ain't just about pushing wands. Sometimes it gets messy."

"Messy is when a baby eats and gets food all over themselves. Messy is leaving dirty dishes in the sink for a couple days. That wasn't messy. It was fucking disgusting," Reggie said.

A couple of people in the room chuckled, but everyone was looking at Reggie who remained stone-faced.

"Y'all need to start writing notes on these weirdos in the customer section," he said.

"Did you?" Henry asked.

Reggie stared at Henry but said nothing in response.

"Exactly. Because you need someone to have that first time experience like you did. Truth is if we told you, his apartment would never get cleaned. He ain't a difficult man. Just fucked in the head. No telling what he saw or did that made him that way, but he's still a man," Henry said becoming serious over the course of his speech.

There was a respect for Henry that permeated throughout the company. He was older than everyone at the shop, even the managers, but he had earned his respect through years of hard work. He could be tough if you were on his van, but he was fair. A southern Black man who loved his whiskey and had more than one story about the women who sat nude on the couch watching him clean when he first started at the company.

"Yeah, well, next time you clean up all that shit and tell me what's left of the man," Reggie responded.

He clocked out for the day and left.

CHAPTER 5

Waking up from his nap, Reggie decided to walk to Smiley's for a beer.

The day was warm. Activity around the motel was scattered. He heard the rattle of the trunk from whoever was playing loud music on the front side of the building. A noise he'd grown accustomed to since staying at the motel.

Reggie smelled the meat from the taco truck as soon as he opened his door.

"What's up big bruh?"

Reggie looked over and saw Money as he stepped out of his room. He had his bike flipped upside down and was oiling the chain. He used the rolling chair from the room to sit on. A half-empty bottle of Miller High Life sat on the ground next to him.

Even though Money called Reggie big bruh, Money was older by at least ten years. Reggie noticed this but never said anything.

"What's going on M?" Reggie said.

"Shiid, I can't call it. You heard them shots last night?" he asked.

Money was good for news and general happenings in the area. He rode up and down the streets on his bike and was even on foot some days. He saw a lot and remembered faces. He'd either taken a liking to Reggie or maybe it was just their proximity. But Reggie didn't pose a threat and he was a consistent customer. Dealers respected loyalty.

"Shots? Gunshots? I didn't hear anything last night I was knocked out. What time?" Reggie asked.

"It was late, but anyway they was chasing each other. I was sitting on my bike in the cut by the sto'. It was a black car and a red car. The guy in the black car let off three shots towards the red car. Pap. Pap. Pap. Guy in the red car shot back twice. They zoomed down the street chasing after each other. I heard two more shots and then shit got quiet," Money said and sat back in his chair.

Reggie was taking in the story. Money had been gesticulating throughout. His hand gestures made it seem like one of those shootouts from the wild west. The silver lining, ironically, was that at least this seemed personal. Madcap gunslingers be damned.

"I missed all of that," Reggie said.

"I went to my other spot after that. They made it too hot over here with all that gunplay. But I ain't heard nobody talking bout it so I'm guessing nobody got hit," Money said.

"They both lucky then," Reggie said.

"Lucky? Unless they see each other again. Can't walk around knowing a man tried to kill you. That ain't over with," Money said.

Reggie shook his head. He hadn't missed much it seemed.

"I got some new fuego if you need it," Money said as he put his index and thumb to his mouth to let Reggie know he meant weed.

"I'm good right now," Reggie said.

"Aight. Don't wait too long. This new shit is pressure. Prolly only last a few days," Money said.

Reggie nodded and trekked downstairs.

A lady in her early 40's stepped out of her room. Reggie had guessed her age since seeing her when he first moved in. Still in great shape, today she wore a patterned silk scarf, yellow tank top, and red spandex.

Reggie nodded to her. She smiled back and proceeded to sweep away the dirt from in front of her door.

He never understood this, but maybe it was her way of protecting her sanity in this hell hole. Like being able to clean up her surroundings gave her a sense of control. Because if she couldn't control her situation, she could control what happened to her in that situation.

The Indians who owned the motel were making their rounds cleaning the rooms and putting out any tenants who hadn't paid their $65 for the day. He'd established a quiet civility with one of the younger Indian men in the office. He'd heard his name called in the lobby but hadn't gotten it from him officially. Isaac. They nodded as they passed one another.

"Hey, how are you doing?" Isaac said without pause.

"I'm good, man," Reggie said not expecting him to speak.

"That's good man," Isaac said.

The young Indian man knew Reggie paid his rent on time and wasn't a bother. They'd spoken on occasion but mostly acknowledged one another through nonverbal communication.

Reggie pulled his cap close to his eyebrows and continued to the mini-mart.

❄ ❄ ❄

"Hi, you!"

The voice belonged to Chinedu, the Nigerian lady who owned Smiley's Mini-Mart. The outside was rundown, but the inside was clean and they kept the shelves stocked. Chinedu looked to be in her mid-fifties. She was missing the top two back teeth on both sides of her mouth but smiled often nonetheless.

Reggie did hear her go off on school kids occasionally, but only when they tried to steal. She never called the cops. Only gave them a tongue lashing and told them to *Get the fuck out of my store!* in her thick Nigerian accent. She was eating peanuts in a Ziploc bag when he entered. She finished cracking one that was in her hand and sealed the bag.

"How you doing today Chinedu?" Reggie asked.

"Hot. Today the temperature is crazy," she responded as she finished chewing.

"Yeah, I know. May have to take a shower when I get back to the room."

She giggled, "Oh, I know. One minute rain, then hot as ever. Where's the cold?" Chinedu said wiping the peanut residue from her face.

"Right. I don't know if I'm taking it off or putting it on," he replied.

She laughed hard and covered her mouth as she did so. Reggie knew it wasn't that funny, but figured it may have been her first time hearing the line. Or maybe she just liked the joke. She was a jovial woman most of the time he'd been in the mart.

"That's a good one," she said and finished laughing.

Reggie walked over to the beer section of the coolers. He grabbed two Ice House 42 ounces, a bag of salt and vinegar chips, and headed for the register.

"How you been?" Reggie asked.

"I've been alright. Can't complain," she said.

She watched Reggie from behind the glass at the register.

"I hear that," Reggie said.

"How bout you? How you been?" Chinedu asked.

She rang up his beer as they spoke. The door chimed as a customer walked into the mini-mart.

"Work keeps me busy," Reggie said.

He turned and watched the woman who had entered walk to the coolers and turned his attention back to Chinedu.

"Oh, trust me. I understand. But just be glad you're still able to work," Chinedu said.

"Fair enough," he said.

Small talk. They never got into any personal matters, just friendly conversation between two passing strangers. Although he'd been coming to the mini-mart for the past few months, he had never told her his name. Everyone knew her and her husbands' name because they were the owners and ran the mart regularly. He'd never offered his name nor did she ask. Small talk between strangers. He found it funny how you could know someone, but never truly know a damn thing about them. At least none of the important stuff. He liked things that way. Preferred it honestly.

Back in the room, Reggie smashed a roach on the wall with his shoe. The low but audible crunching sound satisfied him every time he did so. He cleaned the roach off the wall with a piece of tissue and tossed it in the trash can.

He made a game out of killing them when he was drunk. Every kill felt like a year had been added on to his life.

Sports Center was on in the background. He was only moderately interested at this point. He scanned the room for more of his amigos to kill. None were in sight.

Sometimes he went days without seeing one, those were good days. But, as every Black man knew and in these times every person for that matter knew, there was always some bullshit right around the corner.

Sunday. The last day of a weekend that always seemed to go by too fast. Reggie had a slight headache from the beer the night before. Cheap beer usually gave the worst headaches but yielded the most spirit on a budget. It wouldn't be as bad if he cared for the rule of drinking water before, during, and after imbibing his beer, but why waste the drunk he figured.

He needed to do laundry today. He'd try to go early before too many people packed the laundromat connected to Smiley's. It too was run by Chinedu and her husband. They unlocked the door as soon as they opened the store in the morning. They usually wouldn't go into

51

the laundromat after unlocking the door unless there was a problem with one of the machines. Which usually only meant one of the washers or dryers ate someone's coins. It basically ran by itself. Do your laundry and leave. Some of the locals took advantage of the fact that they didn't closely monitor activity in the laundromat and made drug deals in the bathroom, but, other than that, nothing really happened.

He threw his dirty work clothes in a large clear garbage bag that he got from the maid and walked to Smiley's to exchange a ten-dollar bill for a roll of quarters to use for the machines. He had a bottle of liquid detergent in the room so he didn't have to buy any today. He was thankful for this. Detergent was expensive on a budget so he kept the cups small and tried to stretch his bottles as far as he could.

There was a black Camry parked on the side of the building. He walked in and saw a Mexican man sitting in one of the seats that lined the main wall in the laundromat. The man looked up briefly when Reggie entered. They nodded to one another in acknowledgment and went back to minding their business. Reggie looked in the washers until he saw an empty one and stopped in front of it.

There was an old Pac-Man machine in the back that separated the side with the washers from the side with the dryers. The laundromat was, wall-to-wall, not much bigger than his room at Competitive. When it was crowded it could give you the feeling of claustrophobia, but, after encountering a packed laundromat the first time he'd done his laundry, Reggie had figured out the times and days when he could do his laundry with the least amount of people around.

He placed his quarters in the slot before putting in his clothes. He poured in his detergent and pushed the slot to slide the quarters in after. He observed the washer fill with sudsy water from his liquid detergent and took a seat.

Reggie got a full spectrum of the area while doing his laundry. Though mostly Mexicans came in, Blacks and Whites were also in the mix. He'd see a lowly pimp from time to time as well. Lowly because their women weren't much to look at. Crackheads at best. But what a man would stick his dick in didn't surprise Reggie. After a few brews or a couple tokes of the ganja, anything was possible. And some of the men would be on something stronger than either of those anyways. They had no shame. He'd been asked on more than one occasion for $5 to spot one of the customers so they could relieve their stress. He'd said no each time. Not because he cared that they'd be copulating prostitutes, but because he didn't care to part with his money for the cheap thrills of others.

He sometimes went back to the room while his clothes were washing. He only did this because the washers locked. Otherwise, he'd stick around until he finished both washing and drying. Theft was common in laundromats or *lavandería's* as was the common name posted on laundromats in the area because of the large population of Mexican's. There were a lot of homeless men and women in the area, but the owners made a point of shooing them away. They'd been getting complaints from customers of threatening-looking men standing around the building. The owners knew they weren't threatening, just homeless. But business was business. One or two would wander up and stand for a while before being made to leave, but they'd all gotten the message after so many times and eventually stopped coming.

He decided to sit and wait on his clothes. He was in no rush.

CHAPTER 6

"Can I ask you something?"

Reggie looked over at Dustin who he'd assumed was asleep. Assistants had the luxury of sleeping on the way to and from jobs if they chose to. Probably the only thing Reggie missed about being an assistant.

The sky was gray and filled with clouds. Reggie hadn't checked the weather, but he knew it'd be raining by the time they got to the second house.

"What?" Reggie responded not taking his eyes off of the road.

Dustin had arrived late to the shop and Reggie had had to wait on him before beginning the day. He hated starting late because it usually meant staying out longer, but he'd calmed down after eating his turkey footlong from Subway. His breakfast choice at least two mornings out of the week.

"How long you think you gon' be working here?"
Dustin asked.

The thought had never occurred to Reggie. He
acted on instinct. Surviving on a day-to-day basis meant
dealing with the issues directly in front of him. Fair Zone
was the only thing between him and sleeping under a
bridge in Uptown with the other homeless men he saw a
few times a week.

"What do you mean?" He asked.

"I mean how long you see yourself staying at Fair
Zone. Long term."

"As long as the check clears or I get a better
paying job is the simple answer. The only answer really,
right?" Reggie said.

Dustin thought about Reggie's answer.

"I'm not in a rush, ya know?" Reggie said trying
to clarify his answer.

"Fair enough," Dustin responded.

"Why you asking that question anyway? You just
got here. Already thinking bout leaving?" Reggie
prodded.

"I've heard talks around the shop about the slow
season coming up. If what I'm hearing is true, I gotta
figure something else out. I'm new and haven't made
enough to survive that type of a pay cut."

"It's hard for people who've been with the
company for years. Being new don't have anything to do
with it. But I understand your point," Reggie said.

Though he was only thirty-two, Reggie had ten years on Dustin. He could hear the ambition of being in one's early twenties in Dustin's voice.

"How bad is it?" Dustin pressed.

This year would be Reggie's second time experiencing what they considered the slow season at Fair Zone. It lasted from early January until the beginning of April.

Everyone got their carpet cleaned for the major holidays at the end of the year: Thanksgiving, Christmas, and right after New Year's. After that, people generally didn't care to have their carpets cleaned the first few months of the year.

It had been rough. And with Reggie's living situation, it had become damn near unbearable. But he'd managed to pull off enough side jobs when they did get scheduled to clean to scrape by with rent, food, and was still able to afford his bad habits of beer and weed. Not much beyond that though.

He'd been thinking about the slow season for the past few weeks. Saving was out of the question. Fair Zone didn't pay enough for him to have rainy day funds and he found he was too tired when he got off to work a second job.

"I'll tell you like they told me. Stack your bread these last couple months. You're gonna need that money after New Year's," Reggie said. He knew he was lying, but it felt right to say nonetheless.

They were stopped at a red light and Reggie was staring at Dustin as he spoke.

"That or get a second job," Reggie added.

Dustin grimaced. He didn't like the idea of working two jobs.

"Hopefully I can get one solid job before then. Cause fuck that. I'm not working two jobs," Dustin said flatly.

"I definitely understand that," Reggie said.

The light turned green and Reggie drove to their first house of the day.

❄ ❄ ❄

Rhonda was thick. She answered the door wearing only a shirt that ended just under the cuff of her behind.

Dustin was taken aback when she answered the door. Reggie guessed her age to be in the mid-forties range. Pretty, but missing the attention of a man. He could tell she was single by her attire. He'd seen enough of this behavior to notice the pattern.

The job was a redo. She'd gotten the stairs and living room cleaned the first time around but hadn't liked how the carpet cleaned up.

Larry and another assistant were the original cleaners. Larry tended to rush through jobs. He didn't care about being thorough. He just wanted to get in, get paid, and leave. There were complaints from customers, but Chris would only tell Larry to slow down; there weren't any real consequences.

Fair Zone allowed redo's up to 48 hours of the original cleaning. Free of charge of course and Rhonda had taken advantage of that policy.

They were standing in the living room and Rhonda was pointing out problem areas that she thought should have been cleaned more thoroughly.

She walked to the steps and started making her way up, pointing out stains as she did so.

Reggie was only half-paying attention. All he could focus on was the fact that she was walking up the stairs wearing a white t-shirt that came down to her mid-thigh. Her thong on full display.

She continued walking and speaking as normal.

He looked back at Dustin to confirm what he was seeing. Dustin nodded and turned back to the show.

"Alright," Rhonda said as she reached the top of the stairs and turned to face the two men. "That's all I have for you. I have to clean my bathroom so you can get started where you like and come get me if you have any questions," she said.

"Okay. We'll get set up and get to work," Reggie said.

❄ ❄ ❄

Reggie started cleaning at the top of the steps and worked his way down.

The bathroom was directly in front of the stairs. Rhonda was bent over cleaning the tub the entire time Reggie was in view.

He knew she knew he could see everything and didn't care. She had even gazed back at him and smiled.

Dustin was downstairs in the living room and saw none of this. Reggie relayed what he'd seen on the drive back to the shop. Dustin was more upset that he hadn't told him to come see the show.

Reggie glanced up a few times as he made his way down but didn't give her much attention otherwise.

The current vibes in the country were too fragile. Although he did appreciate the show, people's ulterior motives were questionable.

He finished cleaning and they left shortly after.

※ ※ ※

His prediction of rain proved true. The rain started while they were packing up the van after they finished cleaning Rhonda's home. Not exactly at the second house, but close enough.

Reggie hated when it rained. The hoses would get wet so they'd need to carry blankets from the van to lay them on the floor so as not to bring excess water into the customer's home. They'd also need to pocket extra shoe covers so they didn't track mud onto newly cleaned carpet or floors in general. They had both grabbed company rain jackets before leaving the shop.

Reggie backed into the driveway of the next house. The hoses were run from the back of the van so while backing in wasn't necessary, it made the job much easier.

Parked, he checked the tablet in silence. Dustin stared out at the rain. He already had his jacket on. Reggie finished reading the Client History and put his jacket on as well.

"You ready?" Reggie asked.

Dustin said nothing, but nodded that he was ready.

Reggie grabbed the tablet from its charging station in the van, Dustin grabbed the chip bucket from beside him and they exited the van.

❋ ❋ ❋

A middle-aged Black man answered the door. Reggie recalled that the name of the homeowner who booked the job was a female so he figured this must be her husband.

"How's it going? I'm Reggie."

"Wassup Reg."

"This is my assistant Dustin," Reggie said.

"How you doing," Dustin said.

"Can't complain."

"Got some work for us today?" Reggie asked.

"Yeah, come in," he said stepping to the side to welcome the two men in. "My girlfriend, Rita put in for the cleaning. She'll be out in a second, but I know it's the living room and the master bedroom for sure." The man said.

"Yeah, I saw in the tablet it's two rooms and a hallway," Reggie said.

61

"Okay then. Yeah, it's those two rooms and the hallway right there," the man said pointing towards the hallway. "She may want y'all to clean her daughter's room as well, but I'll let her tell it when she comes out. Y'all can just get started in the hallway and the living room for now. She should be done getting ready by then," the man said.

The man seemed pretty even. His suspicions about the man being the husband were proven wrong as he had heard him refer to her as his girlfriend. Men moving in with women was the thing of modern times. Seemed a lot of women were making more than their male counterparts in the workforce.

"Alright, cool," Reggie said.

He got him to sign the slip and fall notice.

"You guys drink beer?" The man asked handing the tablet back to Reggie.

It wasn't noon yet. Not that that bothered Reggie, but he wasn't going to drink with a customer. That opened the door to all kinds of trouble.

"Yeah, but I'm good," Reggie said.

"You sure? What about your assistant?" He looked over at Dustin, "You want a brew, boss?"

Reggie could tell Dustin was considering taking one by the look on his face.

"I'm good," Dustin said finally.

"Aight. I gotta run to the store. Y'all can go ahead and do ya thing. I won't be gone long. Just knock on the door if y'all got any questions. Rita should be able to hear you knock from the bathroom."

"Got you," Reggie said.

The man grabbed his keys from atop the counter and left.

"Pretty hospitable," Dustin said.

Reggie looked at Dustin but didn't speak. He only nodded in recognition of his comment. They both headed to get the van set up and start the job.

❄ ❄ ❄

The rain had begun coming down harder. Reggie and Dustin did their best to keep the hoses as dry as possible, but they still got wet. The amount of rain made it impossible to keep them completely dry.

Luckily there was more grass than dirt in the yard, so they didn't have to worry about tracking mud into the house. Reggie had experienced this while he was an assistant. The entire cleaning was a shit show and the homeowners ended up scheduling a redo for the next day.

Maybe he would take a beer to go he thought to himself as the rain bounced off of his jacket.

❄ ❄ ❄

"Tacos?" The Mexican lady on the food truck asked.

"Yes," Reggie replied.

"How many?"

"Two."

"Steak?"

"Yes."

A familiar dance. She smiled, turned, and dumped a container of steak on the grill. She squirted oil from a clear bottle onto the meat while chopping and stirring it with her spatula.

He was glad the truck stayed open until 11 pm most nights. He'd have to eat shitty gas station food if not(though he only found the microwaveable food to be bad). He watched her make the tacos. Her hips swung as she moved from the grill to the section where she kept the toppings.

She looked back at Reggie. "7 minutes."

He nodded and smiled.

He turned from the truck, looked around, and caught a drug deal going on across the street at Smiley's. There were still patrons going in and out of the store.

"Yo, you need a crockpot?"

Reggie turned.

A haggard man, front teeth missing, clothes ragged with a cast on one foot was staring at him. He held an unopened crockpot and smiled the smile of every child missing their front teeth.

"I'm good boss," Reggie said.

"You sure? Brand new. Ain't even been out the box."

Reggie could see the spit flying through the space in his teeth as he spoke.

"Nah. I'm good," he repeated.

"Aight. You could stop buying these expensive ass tacos from these cholos. You know if this was a soul food truck they wouldn't buy shit from yo' black ass, right?"

Old head probably got a point he thought to himself. But, he still wasn't interested. That pot would be a cesspool for the vermin currently residing in his room. He respected the hustle though. At least he had more to offer than an empty hand hoping for the kindness of others.

"I'm good o.g. Maybe some other time."

"Aight. Just tryna give you the real," he said.

Reggie stared as the man limped to the street. He waited for a car to pass before crossing.

"Green sauce or red sauce?"

The Mexican lady broke his stare.

"Green sauce," he said.

❋ ❋ ❋

Reggie was awoken by the blare from ambulances, police sirens, and a fire truck.

Groggily, he made his way to the lone window in his room and glanced out of the curtain. Four cop cars and an ambulance were parked downstairs. The fire truck sounded like it just pulled in and was making its way around the building.

Reggie heard crying and shouting. A male voice produced this commotion. He headed to his door and opened it.

"What's up big bruh?"

Money stood at the railing observing the action smoking a cigarette.

"What's good Money?"

"I can't call it," Money said while taking a drag of his cigarette.

"The fuck going on downstairs?" Reggie asked.

"Ion know yet. From what I can tell doh', somebody dead," Money said.

"Word?" Reggie asked.

"Hell yeah," Money said.

"I told her to stop taking those pills! Told her!" The cries echoed through the complex.

"Ain't that New York?" Reggie asked rhetorically.

"Hell yeah. I think it's his old lady that done checked out," Money said.

"Oh, shit. They just got here a few weeks ago," Reggie said.

"Hell yeah," Money quiets to a whisper. "I done sold to both them muh-fuckas too. They better not mention my fucking name. I ain't got shit to do with these crackheads dying. I'm just tryna make my money and stay out the way. Feel me?" Money asked looking for validation.

"I feel you, my dude," Reggie responded.

Money nodded. Pleased with the agreement.

The two men stood in silence. The lights from the emergency vehicles lit the side of the complex up like the fireworks at Epcot. Money took drags from his cigarette.

Nothing happening at this point, Reggie started getting drowsy again.

"Well shit. I'm bout to get some more sleep. I'mma holla at you. Let me know if you find out what happened," he said.

"Aight big homie," Money said and took a pull of his cigarette. "Put a word in for me at that job."

"Put in an application," Reggie responded as he shut his door.

Money rolled his eyes.

CHAPTER 7

"I'm sure you've all heard about the death that happened yesterday at Global."

Chris stood at the front of the room addressing the Fair Zone employees. His face was solemn.

Unlike Fair Zone, Global Cleaners was a chain carpet cleaning company. They were Fair Zone's main competition in the city, but Fair Zone had managed to establish enough of a customer base to stay in business and compete with the larger chain.

"Young kid. Only 18. He backed the van into the garage and was overcome by the carbon monoxide that got pumped into the house. Found him dead in the master bedroom," Chris said scanning the room.

"Well, shit," Henry said in a low voice.

"That's why we stress that you all never do this. And make sure you're using the door seals that should be in all of your vans. I want all crew chiefs to check your van before leaving base and make sure you have a door seal. We're going to be making rounds the next few days and if there's no seal in the door when we pull up, expect that to be your last day at Fair Zone," he said.

Everyone's eyes shifted from each other back to Chris.

"Accidents happen, but we prevent what we can. I don't plan on making any calls to any of your family about a dead cleaner."

These last remarks sounded insensitive, but Reggie could tell that Chris meant well. He'd heard Chris say CYA several times. Cover Your Ass.

"Other than that, it's business as usual today, fellas. Be thorough in your cleaning and mind the roads," Chris said. "Grab a couple Gatorade's out of the laundry room before you leave and have a great day today guys," he said.

Everyone got up and headed to their vans.

❄ ❄ ❄

Reggie and Dustin, just finished cleaning the scheduled rooms in the tablet, were standing in the kitchen talking to Orlando Johnson. He'd gotten his carpets cleaned every three months. His birthmark, which looked like a half-moon, was next to his right eye.

"How much y'all charge to clean those two little rooms in the back?"

Reggie knew he'd ask.

"You got cash?"

"How much?" Orlando responded.

"$50," Reggie said.

"Done. Come get me when y'all through. I'll be in the back messing around with shit."

Orlando left through the back door. Reggie and Dustin lugged the equipment into the back bedroom.

"It's kind of insane isn't it?" Dustin asked as Reggie connected the steam hose to the wand.

"What's crazy?" Reggie asked.

"How comfortable people are with total strangers being in their home," Dustin said handing Reggie the vacuum hose.

"They don't consider us strangers. They think of us as employees. That covers their ass. Not ours. Anything happens, they'd just put in a complaint with the company," Reggie said as he used the vacuum hose to suck up the food crumbs that had settled near the baseboard.

"I guess that's true," Dustin said thinking about Reggie's remark.

"I know it is. Customers are always looking for a free cleaning. Even if we get fired in the process," Reggie said.

Reggie walked to the furthest corner of the room to start cleaning. He learned to do this while working with Henry during his first week with the company. You'd always have enough hose if you started in the furthest corner and worked your way out of the room.

"Remember to leave me enough hose to hang myself with!" Reggie shouted over the sound of the wand once he'd connected the hose. He'd learned that phrase from Henry as well. A funny way of letting the assistant know not to pull too much hose out of the room. The constant tug got annoying and slowed the cleaning process.

Dustin stood near the doorway looking at the pictures of Orlando with his wife, son, and daughter on the dresser closest to the door. The children looked to be no older than three and five. He watched Reggie to make sure he didn't need to pull hose, but he studied the room in between glances.

His back turned to Dustin, Reggie didn't pay him any mind.

Dustin eyed the jewelry box sitting atop the main dresser in the room. It was a wooden jewelry box. 10" in height with a smooth top that lifted up. There were two drawers in the front. He pulled some of the hose out of the room and moved closer to the dresser. He stared at the box.

"Turn the suction down!" Reggie yelled.

Dustin snapped out of his stare. He turned to Reggie who had been watching him after he zoned out.

"What?" Dustin asked.

Reggie disconnected the hose and placed the end on his leg to muffle the sound.

"Turn the suction down. I'm gonna rip this carpet up with how hard my wand is pulling. The carpet needs to be tacked back down in here. Remind me to mention that to Orlando if I forget," Reggie said.

"I got you," Dustin said as he turned and left.

Reggie waited until he was gone and then glanced down at the jewelry box. He didn't see anything special about it. Nor did he see anything special about anything in the room for that matter. He shrugged it off and reconnected the hose.

He drug the wand back and forth on the carpet. The tug was noticeably less. He started cleaning again.

❄ ❄ ❄

They made $150 on the day in side job money. Reggie stopped by a 7-Eleven to gas up and break one of the $50 bills so he could give Dustin his $75 before returning to base.

Reggie closed the door to the gas tank and climbed back into the van. Dustin was counting his money.

"See this makes the job not so bad," Dustin said as Reggie settled into his seat. "If we could do this every day that'd be almost an extra $400 a week."

"How long you been here?" Reggie asked.

"Six months," Dustin replied.

"Then you already know this doesn't happen every day. Hell, some days we don't even get tip money. We just work whatever's in the tablet and that's it," Reggie said sipping the blue Powerade out of his Big Gulp cup he'd purchased when he went into the gas station.

"I know. I'm just saying it'd be nice is all," Dustin said. "It's already November. What'd you say? Save ya bread? That's what I'm trying to do," he said.

"Why you so hard up for cash?" Reggie asked.

Dustin stared at his feet. He looked up at Reggie suddenly. Reggie saw both confusion and anger.

"Why aren't you?" Dustin said.

"I need money as much as the next man. More even. But it sounds like you're in a tight spot. Like you owe somebody kinda thing," Reggie said.

Dustin was quiet. He stared out the window.

Reggie waited patiently.

"My girl's pregnant," Dustin said after a while.

"How many months?" Reggie asked.

"There's a baby in her belly. That's far enough for me. But three months for sure," Dustin said. His hands were laced and he was twiddling his thumbs.

"That ain't too far along. There's a lot of time for you to save up. And babies aren't that expensive anyway," Reggie said.

Dustin stopped twiddling his thumbs.

"You got kids?" Dustin asked.

Reggie shook his head "No."

73

"Then you don't know a damn thing. Only other job called me besides this one was for a warehouse and they were paying even less than here. $10 an hour. Manual labor for ten fucking dollars," Dustin said.

"Where were you working before?" Reggie asked.

"Bullshit temp agency. They send you somewhere and after 3 months, you need a new job. Nasty cycle to get lost in. I was happy to have a full-time job, but this ain't much better if the money ain't consistent year-round," Dustin said now twiddling his thumbs again.

Reggie could only offer advice. He'd learned that when a man needed money, he didn't care for nor did he take advice.

Reggie didn't have kids, but not because he didn't want any. There were scares, but that's as far as it ever went. And with his situation being what it was, he never questioned his fortune. But he knew Dustin was right. Having children while dealing with financial burdens made a tough existence that much harder.

"You'll be aight," Reggie said. Only half-believing himself now.

Dustin wasn't listening at this point. Reggie turned the key in the ignition and pulled out of the gas station, headed back to base for the day.

❋ ❋ ❋

Back at Competitive, Reggie and Money leaned over the balcony in front of Reggie's door conversing. Money smoked a cigarette as they talked. The nightlife around the motel was tame. Cars pulled in and out and people going and coming into their rooms.

"You figured out what happened?" Reggie asked.

"Hell yeah. New York killed that woman."

Reggie's eyes go wide. "What?"

"Yup. I was talking with Cricket downstairs. He said he heard them arguing in they room last night. They came outside still going at it. "Fuck you. I'on need you muh-fucka" and all that shit. Went back in the room still going off. After an hour or so, he ain't hear nothing so he thought shit was cool. Come to find out this morning that bitch dead."

"Damn, New York," Reggie said.

"Yeah, big bruh. Shit foul."

"How he know New York killed her though and she didn't overdose or something?" Reggie asked.

Money, feeling attacked, didn't like the question. His eyes narrowed as he spoke.

"She had marks around her neck, a black eye, and a gash on her fo'head. I done sold some good shit, but never no shit that beat the fuck out you," Money said.

Reggie laughed at his statement.

"You got that one," Reggie said still laughing.

"So you see what I'm telling you," Money said easing up. "Don't put that shit on me. Everybody grown."

Money took a long drag from his cigarette and flicked it into the parking lot.

"You right. Shit just happen so fast over here man," Reggie said now surveying the parking lot.

"Hell yeah. She was from Charlotte too. Had 3 kids and all. None his so he ain't care nothing about all that. Just another stain on the sheet. Shiid. Now a nigga gone over some bitch. And a bitch gone over some nigga. Shit dumb as hell if you think about it."

Money pulled out his soft pack of Newport cigarettes and plucked one free. He lit it and took a drag. He shook his head in agreement to a comment only known to him while exhaling.

Reggie watched him for a sec.

"You got bud?" He asked breaking the silence.

"How much you need bro?" Money responded snapping out of his daze.

"Just a 20," he said.

Money pulled a bag of weed from his pocket, eyeballed the amount, broke it off, and handed it to Reggie.

Reggie pulled a $20 bill from his pocket and handed it to him. "Good looking Money. Stay safe out here man."

"You too, my nigga."

They bump elbows and Reggie walked into his room.

Money lingered on the railing puffing his cigarette, staring beyond the fence at the passing traffic on the main road.

❊ ❊ ❊

Deborah and Money conversed in their room. They both sipped a 12oz Miller High Life from a six-pack Money purchased at Smiley's.

"They cut my hours at the gas station," Deborah said.

Victoria was asleep in the twin bed closest to the bathroom.

The room was the same size as Reggie's. One of the lights over the bed had a blown bulb. All of the paintings in the room were slightly crooked. The carpet, though clean, was old and faded.

The television was turned to B.E.T. One of the Tyler Perry movies, always in heavy rotation, was on.

"Why the fuck they do that?" Money said sipping his beer.

"Cause they can. Ain't mention nothing. Looked at the new schedule before I left yesterday and was missing 8 hours," she said.

"8? What the fuck?" He said.

"Yup. 2 hours off the 4 days I work a week," Deborah said.

"What the manager say?"

"New store policy. They're cutting back on everybody hours," she said.

"That's some bullshit. They always say shit like that. They bought to hire mo' people, cut y'all hours, and pay theyself," Money said.

Deborah shrugged and polished her beer. Money did the same, grabbed the last 2 out of the pack, popped the top off both, and handed one to Deborah.

"How's looking for a job going?" Deborah asked Money.

"Man, them crackas ain't tryna hire somebody like me. Hard worker or not I been to prison. That shit don't fly in real life. Or they only wanna hire me at some bullshit ass warehouse job making $9 or $10 an hour. They not about to work me to death for that little bit of money" he said.

"I thought you were gonna talk to Reggie about getting a job at that carpet cleaning place?" She asked.

"I did. That man looking out for his self. He ain't fucking with me. I told him to put in a good word for me, but he ain't even wanna do that. All he ever say is "Put in an application."

"Have you?" She asked.

Money stared at her and sipped his beer. He swallowed and set it down on the wooden table.

"Nope."

"Why not?"

"There ain't no point if I can't get help from somebody inside. Them crackas gonna see my felony and throw my application in the trash."

"You sound dumb. How can they hire you or even supposed to know you need a job if you ain't even apply? What the fuck are you doing Bobby?"

Hearing his government name ignited Money.

"What the fuck you mean what I'm doing!?"

A fight was brewing. Victoria, Deborah's daughter, awoke from her sleep.

"I'm making sure YOU and HER got a roof over y'all god damn head. Shit. Maybe you should apply since they cutting your hours. You always pull this bullshit when shit starts fucking up in your life."

"Calm down," Deborah snarled as she noticed Victoria waking up.

"Then stop trying to shit on me all the time. I'm doing the same thing as you. The best I can," Money said.

"I'm not trying to start anything. I'm letting you know we need some more money coming in. This is a fucking motel, Bobby. Not no house. Not even a god damn apartment. I'm not staying here forever," she said

Deborah and Money stared at one another. Victoria, fully awake, sat up in bed.

"Man. Fuck this shit."

Money grabbed his beer and left the room. He slammed the door behind him.

"I don't know why you deal with him. He don't do nothing but yell," Victoria said to Deborah.

"This grown folk business. Go back to sleep," Deborah responded.

Victoria sensed the tension remaining in the room and decided not to add to it.

Relenting, she shook her head and lay back down. Deborah took a swig of beer and stared at the door.

CHAPTER 8

It was a quarter past midnight.

Reggie sat on his bed watching television. He had run out of weed the night before but hadn't seen Money all day to buy more so he settled for a three-pack of Budweiser 24oz beers.

He was halfway finished with his second when someone knocked on the door. The knock was firm and pronounced. Reggie waited to see if it would be followed by another. Two more knocks followed.

The peephole was stuffed with a napkin that had been torn and rolled to fit in the hole. It was too deep to pull out with his fingers and he didn't care enough to fish it out of the hole. He'd need to open the door or look out the window to see who was on the other side of the door. Besides the children who played at the motel and Isaac, no one ever came looking for him.

He sipped his beer and set it down on the rectangular-shaped small wooden table next to the door. He opened the door after.

Two Charlotte Mecklenburg Police Officers stared at him.

Reggie had a small buzz from the beer, but that shook itself loose once he saw the cops. A natural buzz kill.

"How you doing tonight?"

The greeting came from the lead officer.

"Fine," Reggie said.

"We got a noise complaint from one of your neighbors," the lead officer said.

His partner stood behind him observing Reggie the entire time. His hand was balefully placed near his gun. Both were youngish-looking White officers. Though the lead seemed confident enough, his partner looked like he was a bit on edge. Reggie's eyes shifted between the two men.

Reggie was at a loss for a response. *Good thing I wasn't smoking* he thought to himself.

"Something going on in there?" The officer asked looking past Reggie into his room. He didn't see much as he made a wall to wall survey of the room with his eyes.

"Not at all," Reggie said.

"Unwinding a little tonight, huh?" The officer said as he stared at the open can of beer sitting on the table.

"Something like that," Reggie said glancing at his beer.

He stepped aside so both officers could get a full view of the inside of the room. The lead officer waved off the invitation to inspect the room. He glanced inside once more and turned his attention back to Reggie.

"What's your name?" The lead asked.

"Reggie," he said.

"Reggie what?" He asked.

He could tell he was digging for information but continued answering the questions.

"Skinter."

"You have identification?"

"Yes, but what's this all about?" Reggie asked.

The questioning was beginning to annoy him, but he kept his composure. Even though they were public servants, police officers had a reputation for being short-tempered when it came to dealing with minorities. Stories were being run on the news about cops shooting Black people in their own homes after they called for police assistance. These stories were becoming monthly fodder for the media.

"There have been complaints about a sex offender in the area and you fit the description."

Reggie froze in shock. His eyes seemed to bulge out of their sockets. He'd been single awhile but had never been accused of sexually assaulting any woman he'd ever come across romantically or otherwise.

He looked past the lead officer at his partner who was looking sheepishly in another direction to avoid eye contact.

One of the downsides about being in poor areas is that police picked on the dwellers at times. This was one of those times.

Reggie knew they were fishing for information. Innocent, he felt no need to push back. Besides, it would only prolong this forced meeting that was heading downhill fast.

If nothing else, he'd learned through the media's constant showing of violent and deadly interactions between cops and Black men that sometimes it was better to let them move around.

Reggie grabbed his wallet from the nightstand next to the bed and pulled out his license. The officer stood at the door observing him.

He handed him his license and waited.

The officer stared at it for a moment and handed it back.

"Appreciate your cooperation. Just trying to make sure we know who's who out here," the lead said.

"Yeah, I bet," Reggie said.

The officer could hear the sarcasm in his voice but didn't press. He kept the same smug look on his face he'd had when Reggie first opened the door.

"You have a good night," the officer said.

Reggie nodded but didn't speak. Both officers headed down the stairs to return to their squad car. Reggie watched them for a moment and shut the door.

He grabbed his beer from beside the television and downed the remainder.

The police were shit. Bigoted pieces of shit. Not all, maybe, but they seemed to only send the worst ones to mostly Black areas. Always looking to hem up a Black man on trumped-up charges. Or arrest him for drugs that they planted.

Reggie had heard no whispers of a sex offender. If anybody would know, it'd have been Money. And he hadn't mentioned anything to Reggie.

They were fishing.

But Reggie wasn't one of those low-hanging fruits that they made a game of picking up. He was just poor. Not stupid.

That alone made them feel like they could do and say what they wanted with little to no repercussions. Cause poor people had neither the money nor the time to fight against bigot cops.

He'd seen stories on the national news channels regarding encounters with cops and Black people over the past year. Men, women, and children. All violent. Cops mistaking their guns for their tasers. Or at least that was the narrative they'd chosen to run with. Even with all of the body cam footage being released for public consumption. For the most part, they'd ended the same way, someone dead and the cops getting off on some technicality or only charged in the second degree. Mostly White cops, but there was the occasional minority officer involved. Reggie felt that cops that didn't look like those that lived in the neighborhoods they patrolled shouldn't be allowed to patrol those neighborhoods. It's hard to kill Byron or Jasmine and have to bump into their mother at the Food Lion on Monday. But that's just not how things worked in America. Something needed to be done about the level of violence between the cops and the Black community though. Whatever violence was being perpetrated in the Black community aside(and wasn't there violence in all communities?), there was no way those assigned to protect and serve should be allowed to add to the chaos.

"Fuck them," he said aloud and cracked open his last beer.

❄ ❄ ❄

Without fail, every time Reggie rode through an affluent neighborhood, he always imagined himself owning one of the homes.

On any given day, he'd see brick homes, stone homes, homes with vinyl sidings, wooden homes. Homes. Grass. Trees. A yard to call his own. To Reggie, owning a home was consistently on his mind. The fact that he was inside them all the time only added to his desire.

Owning a home wasn't the American dream. Wealth was the American dream, but Reggie would settle

for being able to buy a house. No need to be wealthy to
be able to do that.

In a neighborhood far enough away from
Competitive Inn, he could begin to forget the horrors
he'd experienced since living there.

He also knew that he'd never escape the memories
of poverty. Good or bad, the thoughts of what existence
looked like at the bottom would forever be buried in the
soil of his mind.

❊ ❊ ❊

Another solo day. The sun was out but the day
was chilly and that meant that he wouldn't sweat as
much. At least when he set up and broke down the van.

The first house was empty. There was a storage
unit in the driveway so he figured these were new
homeowners. People liked to clean before moving into a
previously owned home. The key was left in the mailbox
next to the door so Reggie could let himself in.

The house was nice. Two stories, with a ground
pool in the back. The pool was empty but still looked new.

Over time, he had started to look at these empty
homes like crime scenes. He played guessing games of
where the furniture had been and which areas were most
trafficked.

The downstairs had wooden floors, so traffic
patterns were non-existent, but he could see the wax build
up on the floors. He'd learned not to clean wooden floors
using products that promised to make your wood shine

while working at Fair Zone. Chris stressed that wood didn't shine during Reggie's training and that the chemical base in the products that promised this made your floor appear shiny, but the combination of dirt and wax buildup dulled the wood. It could be restored but would be a costly investment depending on how bad the buildup was. Chris followed with a story about charging a woman $3500 to strip the wax from her floors.

They hadn't opted to have the wood cleaned, so Reggie headed upstairs to see how much carpet he'd have to clean.

❄ ❄ ❄

Gambling was just that, a gamble. Most would look at it as irresponsible and, truthfully, it probably was, but he needed the money. Money was a vice. And people did all kinds of things for a quick buck. And piss on people's opinions. It was always easier to look down on the poor and struggling and the ways they invested what little money they could get their hands on. Those that judged didn't contribute to his finances. They only paid lip service. They didn't accept that at any store or gas station he'd ever been to.

Reggie entered Smiley's. He looked towards the counter but didn't see Chinedu's husband. He knew he was working because his burgundy Expedition was parked in front of the store.

No other customers were inside. The door to the manager's office was open. Reggie figured he was attending to some business. He'd usually retreat into the office when foot traffic lightened.

The six-pack was 4.99, but they took out the individual bottles and sold them at .99 cents apiece. A small profit for the store. And Reggie didn't mind. Especially on nights like this where a single was all he could afford.

Chinedu's husband had come out of the manager's office and was standing at the register when he walked up with his beer in hand.

Reggie put his beer on the counter and studied the scratch-offs. Minus the beer, he'd be able to purchase six dollars worth of tickets.

He looked at the $5, $3, $2, and $1 tickets pondering what combination to purchase. He pretended the selection was a game of skill, but it all came down to luck.

Chinedu's husband rang up the beer and waited for Reggie to make his selection. He settled on a $5 "Hit 500" and a $1 "Loose Change" scratch-off.

He handed Chinedu's husband his ten-dollar bill, took his change, and headed back to his room.

❊ ❊ ❊

Back at the room, he cracked the Ice House open and drank deeply. He sat down and stared at the "Hit 500" ticket. It was a number matching game, but there was a 500 symbol that if found you'd win $500 instantly. The jackpot was $200,000, but his luck didn't dictate that he'd hit for that much. He'd settle for the $500 reveal. Honestly, he'd settle for $50, but $500 would give him a head start on his paycheck.

He scratched the $1 ticket first. A bust. He threw the ticket in the trash can. Before scratching the $5 ticket, he took another gulp of beer.

He scratched the four winning numbers first: 16, 43, 8, and 3. He started scratching on the first row left to right. No matches. He scratched the second row left to right. Nothing. He drank more beer.

Reggie scratched one number at a time on the final row: 34, 40, 37, and 9.

He stared at the ticket for what seemed like an hour, but it was only a minute.

Busted.

"Fuck!" Reggie yelled.

He drank more beer and continued to stare at the ticket. Minus the few cents change he'd gotten when he purchased the tickets, he was broke. The downside of gambling.

He'd have to beg his way onto the bus until he got paid on Friday. But this wasn't his first rodeo. He knew how to finagle his bus fare. Hopefully, he could make a few tips in the next couple of days to hold him over.

Reggie threw the ticket away and drank his beer in silence.

CHAPTER 9

Reggie waited outside in front of the entrance to the lobby for his cab to arrive. He didn't like taking cabs because it was expensive. Especially with traffic. The meter ticked slower when the cab was stopped, but it (the meter) never stopped. He'd had to pay $25 one morning for a ride that should have only taken 15 minutes. Charlotte traffic was horrible and getting worse year by year.

He saw Isaac standing in the office. He wasn't paying Reggie any attention. Reggie was surprised to see him this early. Since they lived in the motel, the Indians wouldn't usually be in the office until after 8 a.m. If you rang the buzzer they'd groggily make their way to the desk, but they'd go right back to their room after.

Reggie spotted the green cab turning into the motel. Nite N' Day Taxi was painted in black on both sides and there was a sun and moon logo on the hood and back of the car. Tacky, but it got the point across. He stepped forward so the driver would see him.

He got inside once it pulled up.

❆ ❆ ❆

"Headed to work?" The middle-aged White male cab driver asked.

Reggie was accustomed to this. Most liked to make small talk to pass the time. Some just let the radio fill the silence. They were mostly friendly blue-collar people though.

"Yeah, it's that time again," Reggie responded.

"What do you do for a living if you don't mind me asking," the cab driver said.

"I clean carpets," Reggie said.

He'd responded with *I'm a Carpet Technician* on more than one conversation but it all came down to the same thing. And it cut the question of *What's that?* No need to be unnecessarily fancy with his occupation. He cleaned carpets.

"Really. They pay well?"

"Nah. But they pay every two weeks," Reggie said.

The cab driver laughed. Reggie chuckled with him.

"Man, I been looking for something else to do. They got those new app rides now. I ain't got no vehicle and they fazing us out. These smaller cab companies anyway. I think Yellow Cab should be fine though," the cab driver said.

Reggie knew little to nothing about the cab industry, but the gist was they were being fazed out. He understood that quite clear. Fair Zone had its list of competitors. Global Cleaners was the first one that came to mind.

"Are you guys being affected that quickly? I figured it'd catch on, but I guess I hadn't thought of what that meant for the smaller companies," Reggie said.

"More so because they ain't hired nobody. And they don't pay worth shit here. I had to get the fucking job to hold me over till I could find something else. But ain't nowhere else hiring right now. They got me driving all over town for shit pay all fucking day," the cab driver said.

"I hear ya man. I think it's the same all across the board right now. Well, depending on the kind of jobs you're applying for," Reggie said.

"I got a G.E.D. and I can navigate the internet pretty good. Good enough to get a job anyways. But the type of jobs I can apply to that I can get hired for tomorrow don't pay jack shit. That's just the truth. You see all those commercials about everybody going back to school. I don't want to go back to fucking school. I want the job that I'm good at to pay me a livable wage," the cab driver said.

They rode in silence for a moment. Not because Reggie didn't want to respond. But there wasn't much to say. He didn't control pay and there was nothing he could do for the man. They were all hard up for cash. This man's monologue made that reality no different.

"I'm sorry man. Didn't mean to ruin your morning or anything. It's just bullshit, ya know?"

"It's all good man. I understand. We're about to be in the slow season soon. I still ain't figured out how I'm gonna make ends meet until work picks back up," Reggie said.

"Slow season? For carpet cleaning? I'da thought people needed carpet cleaners year-round," the cab driver said.

"They do. They just need us less the first few months of the year," Reggie said.

"Hmm. Things get slow until around Springtime then?"

"Yes," Reggie said and nodded.

The cab driver saw Reggie nod from the rearview mirror.

"Makes sense," the cab driver said.

"I'd at least tell you to give it a shot, but things would be slowing down right when you started work. I'm not sure how much you make driving cabs, but that might put you in a worse position," Reggie said.

"No, I understand. Hell, I'm just venting really. I honestly don't mind the job. But with pay being what it is and all this new technology, I just don't see how I can afford to keep driving. Guess I'll figure something out eventually," the cab driver said.

"Let me know when you do," Reggie said.

This made the cab driver smile again.

"Is there any station you wanna listen to on the radio?"

"Nah, whatever's fine with me," Reggie said.

The cab driver turned to 99.7 FM. Reggie knew it was the Classic Rock station. He'd listened to it on occasion in his van when he wanted to break up the repetitiveness of the songs he constantly heard on the Hip-Hop stations he listened to on most days at work.

They listened to the radio the remainder of his ride.

❊ ❊ ❊

Reggie and Dustin were cleaning their third house of the day. The homeowner wasn't there but had left a key under the mat so they could complete the service. There were 6 rooms for them to clean in all (three bedrooms, 2 bathrooms, and a hallway). The two-story home was in a neighborhood on the south side of Charlotte.

They were cleaning the tile and grout in the bathrooms first and then the carpets in the bedrooms and hallway.

"You figured out what you gonna do?" Dustin asked.

95

"What I'm going to do about what?" Reggie asked genuinely confused.

"The slow season," Dustin said.

Reggie was scrubbing the grout lines to loosen the dirt. Dustin added more alkaline cleaning solution to the floor as Reggie needed and held the cleaning wand for the tile and grout.

"No," Reggie said. "I'm not looking for another job. I'm just going to have to do what everybody else does. Survive. Unless I hit the lottery," Reggie said.

"You play the lottery," Dustin asked.

"Scratch-off tickets," Reggie said.

"I've tried a few of them. Never won anything. I got up to $20 worth and quit. You either win or lose. No returns on losses. Dangerous to keep taking those types of losses," Dustin said.

"It's only dangerous if you never win. I've won enough to keep me playing. But I ain't delusional. I play more for the smaller cash payouts than I do for the Jack Pot. It'd be nice, but hitting those things are Unicorns," Reggie said.

"Yeah. I knew a guy at my old job who hit. He won $10,000 off a $5 Scratch-Off. Everybody at the job told him to be smart with the money," Dustin said.

Dustin stopped talking and poured more alkaline on the floor.

"Was he smart with the money?" Reggie asked.

"No. He bought a motorcycle and quit. Not sure what happened to him," Dustin.

Reggie stopped scrubbing. He laughed out loud.

"What?!"

"That's what happened," Dustin said now laughing along with Reggie.

Reggie got back to scrubbing the grout lines.

"It'd be nice to hit for that much before the New Year," Reggie said.

"I'm sure it would be," Dustin said.

"What you got planned?" Reggie asked Dustin his own question.

"Still haven't come up with nothing," Dustin said.

"You looking for a second job or another one even?"

"Nope," Dustin said.

Their conversation was going nowhere and they both knew it. They were in the same situation. This conversation was to pass the time more or less.

"You think they got water in the fridge?" Dustin asked.

Reggie shrugged.

"Grab me one if you find any," he said.

Dustin went to check the refrigerator.

Reggie scrubbed the tile. He let the alkaline Dustin poured on the floor settle and then aggravated it into the floor.

"Reggie!" Dustin shouted from the kitchen.

Reggie stopped scrubbing immediately and looked up.

"Yeah!" He shouted back.

"Come here!"

Reggie set the scrubber onto the sink and went to the kitchen.

"What's up," Reggie said when he entered.

Dustin was staring at a wad of money on the counter. The top bill was $100, but he couldn't tell if that was true for the rest of them.

Two water bottles from the refrigerator were sitting on the counter next to the money.

"Where'd that come from?" Reggie asked.

"After I turned around with the water, I saw it sitting here," Dustin said. "How much you think it is?"

"Hard to tell," Reggie said.

He approached the money and looked around instinctually and listened. The house was silent. The two men were the only ones there.

Reggie grabbed the money and ruffled through it. They were all $100's. Reggie looked at Dustin.

"There's a lot of money here," Reggie said.

"You think they'd know?" Dustin asked.

Reggie knew what he meant, but he needed him to say.

"Knew what?" He asked.

Dustin hesitated. He and Reggie shared a knowing glance between the two of them.

"Of course, they'd know," Reggie relented after a moment.

Neither of them needed to say what was understood. Though they both needed the money, this situation was all too good. Even if the homeowner accidentally left the money on the counter, they'd know exactly how much was left. If there was one truth about a lot of wealthy people, they were cognizant of their finances. Plus, they were the only two people in the house. They'd be fired by tomorrow morning at the latest.

Reggie put the money back down.

"Think about it," Reggie said regaining his sense. "What're the odds we get away with this?"

Dustin was thinking about the odds. He knew Reggie was right.

"Would be nice though," Reggie said and grabbed his water from the counter. He downed it and threw the empty bottle in the trashcan.

"Must be nice you mean. I wish I had a wad of money like that to leave lying around," Dustin said.

Reggie shrugged.

"I'm about to finish scrubbing the grout so we can finish the bathroom. We're gonna be here for at least another hour," Reggie said.

He left after.

Dustin stared at the money. He grabbed his water and walked back to the bathroom.

❄ ❄ ❄

The last house was just a hallway. One of their cats had vomited on the carpet. Stomach acid from pets and in general was hard to get up, but it hadn't set nor had it been a bad stain. It took 45 minutes of steam pressing, a citrus solution, and extracting, but he got the entire stain up eventually.

The homeowners were a young couple. The wife was pregnant with what would be their first child. They were excited to tell Dustin and Reggie the news. They had not even told their parents. They were waiting until they saw them the following weekend to relay the news.

Dustin had stood on the side watching the entire time.

Reggie could tell he had been thinking about the money they left behind at their third house. He had been thinking about it too.

They finished up the job and headed back to the shop for the day.

❄ ❄ ❄

"You know we missed out on an opportunity don't you?" Dustin said as the van pulled into the shop

"How so?" Reggie asked.

He parked the van at the entrance.

One of the other technicians, cleaning out his van, waived at the men as they pulled in.

"You think those rich folks woulda missed a few hundred dollars? You think they even counted that money?" Dustin said.

"I don't know what they did with their money. Either way, neither one of us is getting locked up over it," Reggie said. "And look, don't mention seeing money sitting out to none of the guys," Reggie said. "I doubt they'd care, but you don't want your name associated with shit like that. They'd ask what you were doing in the kitchen and all that."

Reggie could tell Dustin hadn't thought of any of what he'd just said. Not that he planned on telling anyone.

"I'm not saying shit," Dustin said.

"Cool. Clean out that trap. I'll park the van when I get out of the office," Reggie said and hopped out of the van after.

Dustin hopped out and went to turn the hose on to rinse out the trap.

CHAPTER 10

The crowd at the Family Dollar was sparse on this early Saturday morning.

It was located off of a busy street near the motel. People stole things constantly and he'd even seen the manager fighting with customers when he first started shopping here. The store was in bad shape. He'd seen a new worker every time he stopped in. Considering the action he'd seen since shopping at the store, he didn't blame anyone wanting to quit. He'd thought about applying so he asked one of the employees about the position. Not to leave Fair Zone, but to have a second income. They told him he'd be starting at $10 an hour and would have to be a cashier for most of his shift. He stopped inquiring after that.

Reggie grabbed a couple of cans of tuna, Beanie Weenies, Vienna sausages, Ramen in a cup, and two six packs of purified water. He headed to the toiletries aisle and grabbed a twin pack of deodorant, body wash, toothpaste, floss, and a new toothbrush. Afterward, he headed to the "Cold Beer" section of the coolers and grabbed two Budweiser 25oz's, and then walked to the register. He grabbed two four packs of Slim Jim's from the "Hot Buy" section near the register.

The cashier, a young Black woman, had a scowl on her face, but he paid her no mind. She finished checking out the Mexican lady in front of him in line. Reggie took his items out of his handbasket and placed them on the slider.

"I'mma start telling people I'm Filipino," the cashier said looking at Reggie.

The remark caught Reggie off guard. He stopped putting his items on the slider and stared at her.

"What?" Reggie said finally.

"I can't be Black no more." She said and leaned in, "Y'all niggas steal too damn much," she said in a tone just above a whisper.

She scanned his Vienna sausages. Reggie just stared not quite sure how to respond. He looked back at the customers in line to see if anyone else heard what she was saying. No one was paying them any attention.

"Even steal cheap cans of meat like this," she said shaking her head.

"Indians are swindlers, Mexicans are drunks, Asians, ironically, don't even like Blacks, and White folks

103

are fucking murderers. Pick your poison. We're all mad here." Reggie said.

He said the words louder than he'd expected. His neck went hot with the eyes of the customers in line behind him now focused on him and the cashier. They stared with wide-eyed expressions. Racial bias was practiced around the world. He made sure her bias wasn't only extended to people whom she resembled.

"Everybody is guilty of something. If they're stealing cheap meat, it's prolly cause they're hungry," Reggie said handing her a $20 bill for his items.

"You ain't steal though," she said.

"I don't need to yet," he said.

He waited for his change and exited the store. Everyone gazed at him.

✻ ✻ ✻

Reggie sat on the edge of his bed guzzling the last can of Budweiser.

He snapped out of his daze, put water in a glad container, placed the container in the microwave, and hit 4. He grabbed a Ramen cup and peeled off the plastic.

Stephen A. Smith was talking about football on ESPN. Reggie didn't care for the sport and wasn't listening to what he had to say.

Bang!

Reggie's door rocked.

Bang!

The door burst open after the second kick.

104

Two masked men stood in the doorway. Reggie, immediately alert, pulled his pocket knife from his jeans and flipped the blade out.

"Get the fuck out!" He yelled at the two men.

Reggie lunged towards them with his knife. Both men recoil. Seeing their timidity gave him confidence. He rushed the door.

"Fuckers! I'll fucking kill you!" Reggie said as he chased them out of the room.

They sprinted down the steps, jumped from the third step from the bottom, climbed the fence next to the motel, and were out of sight a moment later down a path that led to an apartment complex nearby.

No one else was outside.

Reggie waited a minute longer and closed the door.

He pressed 3 minutes on the microwave and squashed a roach as it ran atop the dresser.

There was a knock at the door. Reggie tensed up and waited. Another knock. Knife in hand, he headed to the door and opened it.

Money smiled and shifted his eyes down to his open hand.

"Got some new shit Reg. My guy said it's Blue Dream," Money said.

Reggie didn't care for weed names. Especially once he noticed people were just coming up with shit out of their asses. Call it Possum Fur if you'd like. Weed was weed and right now he just wanted to get high. He was glad Money had stopped by.

He looked past him at the parking lot. Still nobody. Money turned to see what Reggie was looking at.

"What's up, bro? You straight?" Money asked turning back to Reggie.

"Yeah, some young boys kicked in my door," Reggie said.

Money looked left and right puzzled. He looked back at Reggie with the same puzzled look on his face.

"Just now?" Money said.

"Hell yeah," Reggie said.

Reggie was looking around now as well. A feeling of paranoia had begun to settle over him now that he was talking about what happened.

"You aight?"

"Yeah, they weren't on nothing. Just trying to get an easy lick. That's it," Reggie said.

"You know where we at Reg. Just make sure you watch your six out here bro. Get you a gun if you need to," Money said.

Reggie had never owned a gun. He'd bought his knife from Wal-Mart a couple of years ago, but, besides using it at work sometimes, he'd never pulled it on a person. It did make him feel good to have, but he was now wondering if he didn't need something that would keep a little space between him and the unhinged men roaming the streets.

"Hold up," Reggie said and shut the door. He grabbed $20 out of his wallet and returned.

"I'll do 2 for $20 for ya bro," Money said.

"Bet," Reggie replied.

Money pulled out his bag of weed, eyeballed two grams, and handed it to Reggie.

"Good looks my dude," Reggie said.

"You know I got you," Money responded.

The microwave beeped in the background. Reggie shut the door and headed to pour the hot water into his cup noodles.

I gotta get the fuck away from here he thought to himself as he poured.

❄ ❄ ❄

The weekend had been a bust. It was Sunday and with all of the commotion, Reggie had been more on edge than anything. He hadn't been able to sleep from the situation the night before. He didn't try. He kept thinking they may come back. If they did, he'd be ready. He kept his knife right beside him as he sat up in bed throughout most of the night.

There was nothing to do today. He had no errands to run. Sunday's could be days like that. Just waiting for Monday so you could get the week over with again.

As long as he could escape whatever violence that may be happening around him, he'd be thankful for that. He wasn't picky about his good or bad days.

He'd gotten up to look out of his door several times. He hadn't seen Money on either occasion. He stood outside and took in the winter air for a bit and returned to his room. It was a lazy Sunday. He would probably nap on and off throughout the day.

Other than that, it just depended on what came his way. He didn't have much money most of the time so he wouldn't go out looking for something to do. He didn't care to go downtown as that had gotten repetitive after awhile.

Isaac and the other Indians were either in the office or in their room. It'd been a couple of days since he'd last seen him. And that was fine. They needn't see one another. Truthfully, they didn't have anything to talk about between the two of them and wouldn't know one another if Reggie hadn't been staying in the motel.

He had seen the older lady outside her room the first time he stepped outside. She wasn't sweeping or doing anything in particular. She, like Reggie, seemed to be taking in the early morning air.

He thought about going downstairs to speak but decided against it. She didn't look like she cared to be bothered and he wasn't in the mood to force conversation. But she was pretty. There was a million ways she could have ended up here, but outwardly she seemed to have things together.

But he knew stories, real ones at least, weren't wrapped in neat bows. He was sure this outward look of humility had been gained and was probably being gained through tremendous stress and pressure.

He observed as she stared out at nowhere and nothing. Taking in the day before it had a chance to load its' gun. *Good for her* he thought and meant it. Hopefully, she was able to figure it out enough to get away from the motel. Though she might be able to find herself here at the bottom, this was no place to try and build a life. Life started after. If she got stuck here, she'd never make it. Not because she wasn't strong enough, but because you simply cannot thrive in all environments.

Reggie observed her for a bit longer and headed back inside his room.

The night was winding down on his weekend. Reggie sat up in bed with his back against the wall. Besides his shoes, he was fully dressed. He hadn't slept as he thought he might. He could only think of his current state.

Motivation was everywhere around him, but like fool's gold, it was also a depressant. Constantly being surrounded by poverty took a toll on him. He could suppress it at work and by keeping his mind occupied, but it was never far from his thoughts. He wanted nothing more than to get away for good. He thought about Dustin and the unborn child that was already a burden. *Maybe I was wrong for telling him not to take the money* the thought came to him.

And maybe he was. He needed the money just as much. And rich people or people with enough money to leave $100's lying around by accident couldn't need the money as much as he and Dustin. They couldn't begin to understand what men in their shoes had to put up with to make their daily bread.

The slow season loomed and he still didn't have any plans for extra money.

His thoughts were coming all at once and were making him feel claustrophobic in the room. He hopped off the bed and left the room for air.

He felt relieved as soon as he felt the night air. Confined spaces heightened depression. Or at least he thought so. The feeling that he was alone and everything was crashing down pushed him further into himself.

Standing outside, he remembered that there was life being lived outside of and, more importantly, regardless of his circumstances. Life moved on. He always needed to remind himself of that. The realization didn't change what he was dealing with. Only he could do that.

There were three cars in the parking lot. No surprise. He walked to the edge of the railing to see if Smiley's was still open. The Open sign was still flashing in the window. He could just make out Chinedu's husband's burgundy Expedition. Other than that, their parking lot looked deserted as well.

He secretly hoped that the woman downstairs would step outside. Not because he was developing a crush on her, he liked her energy. But he knew she would not be stepping out. He never saw her outside her room after dark. She was smart. Nothing good happened at or around the motel after dark.

CHAPTER 11

"I'm so sorry Missy."

She slapped her Damon across the face. She'd come up with the term to replace the John's she slept with when she first got started. Breanna Miles, late twenties, worldly, well put together, and a gypsy attitude towards life. She had an heir about herself. Not that she felt that she was better than anyone, but she was comfortable in her skin. She was a prostitute when she first got into the life but had stopped walking the streets not long after finding out she could make much more money by having regular Damon's and not John's. John was aggressive. They all had energy that they needed to get off. Good or bad. She'd been on the receiving end of more bad energy than she cared to remember. She never took a beating. None of the men she'd dealt with were punchy. And she had every intention to defend herself if any ever were. But she'd known girls that had gotten punched on pretty bad by some of their John's. But Damon's were weak. She got her energy off on them. Damon needed to be dominated.

Missy. That's what she told her Damon's to refer to her as. She'd never given her real name. Even when she was working the streets. She went by "Bonnie" when she first started as a streetwalker. Everyone wanted to be her Clyde. She got a laugh out of it every time. Because Clyde was gay. Funny how everybody skipped that fact when they romanticized the pair. She learned over time that it was best never to romanticize anything. She found romanticism to be one of the biggest lies of modern life.

The hotel wasn't too fancy. Tucked away on the west side of Charlotte, it was nice enough that she didn't worry about being robbed, but inexpensive enough to keep a low profile. This was more important for her client base than it was for her. They were the ones paying for the room and whatever accommodations they needed during their appointment.

The police officer's uniform was draped over one of the chairs in the hotel room. He was a middle-aged Asian man. Not her typical clientele. She was used to getting middle-aged and older White men. A Black man would pop up every so often, but, from her experience, Black men didn't care to be beaten or dominated during sex.

"Don't touch me. Ever. Unless I tell you to," Breanna said to the man.

He kept his eyes focused on the ground. She was in complete control.

"Yes, Missy. It won't happen again," the Asian officer said.

She looked down at him. He looked pathetic crouched on the floor in just his tidy whitey's. But these were the men tasked to protect and serve the communities. Inside, they seemed just as primitive in thinking as the criminals they arrested. How ironic that the man who gunned you down might have a pain kink.

It had taken her some time to get used to the life. It helped that she was the one delivering the pain and not on the receiving end. She gained confidence after a while and looked forward to the job on some nights. She got her energy off on Damon on those nights. This was one of those nights.

She struck his back with her cat-o-nine tails. He winced in pain but didn't scream.

"You want another?" She asked seductively.

"Yes, Missy," the Asian officer said.

She struck his back once more. Down on all fours, he breathed rapidly.

"My partner..," the Asian officer began.

She waited for him to continue but he needed to catch his breath. She put her foot under his chin and raised his head.

"Your partner what sissy boy?"

He smiled. He gained confidence in being demeaned.

"He shot someone today," he said. "He didn't die, but he was a Black guy. A dumb punk kid."

He rested his head on her foot. She lifted it again catching him in the throat. He recoiled, but just a bit. She balanced his chin on her foot.

"Why?" Missy asked.

"Why what?" the Asian officer retorted.

"Why did he shoot the kid?"

He sat down Indian-style on the floor. He'd regained some of his dignity as he sat on the floor. Breanna could tell he'd gone from Damon to reliving what he'd seen that day.

She waited for him to tell his story. He hesitated and then looked directly into her eyes. He spoke softly.

"He was scared. That's why. We saw him sitting in his car in an area where he shouldn't have been parked, to begin with. The kid was asleep. My partner tapped on the window and the kid panicked. Partner said it looked like he was reaching for something, but I was watching the whole thing from the passenger side window. He never reached for anything. He didn't even have a chance to react before my partner put two bullets in his chest. Heard that he's gonna make it. They suspended my partner, but that doesn't mean much. He'll

115

be back on the job before the kid gets out of the hospital most likely," the Asian officer said.

Breanna had heard stories like this and worse from her Damon's. Especially the rookie officers. They were the most afraid. She could almost pinpoint which ones would wind up killing someone on the job at some point. They weren't all cops, but a majority were. Some were lawyers, doctors, even start-up company owners. She kept her prices high to discourage the cheaper clients. She'd found that in business in general, people looking for a lot for next to nothing always caused problems. On the street, those problems might lead to death.

"Never seen someone dying. I'm glad he made it, but.. I don't know if I can handle this," he said honestly.

She knew that he felt relieved that he was saying these things to a Black woman. Like that somehow relinquished his involvement. But she wouldn't pass judgment. He wasn't paying for her opinion, nor did she care to get too deep into these things with her clients. That's what they came to her for. To get their punishment for their crimes.

She didn't want to get personal with him so she only listened. The look on his face made him look pathetic to her. She felt sorry for him again at that moment.

Breanna slapped her Damon again. He didn't make a sound but held his face to the side after the slap.

Tonight wasn't a Kumbaya and she couldn't solve his problems. Pain would deal with his guilt as well as any apology could. Better even.

Without a word, he got back on all fours. She struck his back with her cat-o-nine tails several more times.

❉ ❉ ❉

Breanna stumbled onto Competitive Inn looking for a cheap place to stay. She came in the middle of the night with only a bookbag and her purse. She always traveled light. She kept her clothes in rotation. She'd wash them a few times and then buy more and donate the old clothes. With her lifestyle, she needed to be able to pack up and leave quickly. She'd never be able to do that dragging luggage around.

On this night she wore pink sneakers and a burgundy tracksuit. The tracksuit hugged her curves. With her matching pink purse and bookbag, she seemed out of place at the motel. Her hair was pulled back in a ponytail and her natural makeup accentuated her deep complexion.

Isaac noticed her immediately. He studied her as she approached the desk. He'd never seen her at the motel. He'd never seen her on this side of town. She smiled as she approached and held his stare.

He smiled involuntarily as he spoke, "How can I help you?"

"I'd like to pay for the month," she said.

117

Isaac was taken aback. Nobody ever paid for a month outright. Honestly, anybody who could afford to pay $1200 at one time to stay here was either stupid or desperate. She looked to be neither.

"The month?" he repeated.

"Yes. Is that a problem?" She asked.

He looked her up and down.

"No, no. It's no problem," Isaac said. "What brings you into town?" He asked.

"Business," Breanna said.

He waited for more, but she only looked at him. It wasn't any concern of his and she had no intention of indulging his question. He wouldn't pry as it was none of his business what any of the guests did as long as they could afford their stay. She would have no problem with that.

"Okay," Isaac said.

He was stuck in a half-trance staring at her. She motioned for him to get on with the process of checking her in.

"It'll be $1200," he said finally.

"Y'all take cash?" She asked.

She wasn't stalled in her response.

"Yes and there's no deposit so $1200 even," Isaac said.

Breanna nodded in agreement, opened her purse, and pulled out a wad of money.

Isaac frowned and looked down at the money and then back up at her. Wads of money on this side of town could mean any number of things. It was a telltale sign of drugs or prostitution mostly though.

She counted $1200 in fifties and handed the money to Isaac.

"Can I have your identification?" Isaac asked.

She reached in her purse and pulled out her driver's license.

Isaac grabbed it and looked at it. *Breanna Miles* He said her name in his head. He entered her information into the computer and handed her back her license.

"Smoking or nonsmoking?" He asked.

"Smoking," Breanna replied without hesitation.

She studied the lobby as she waited for Isaac to finish checking her in. There were brochures for attractions around the city and also food menus for restaurants nearby. The lobby wasn't much to look at otherwise. There were a couple of plants that sat on top of the sink towards the back, a unisex bathroom, and an air conditioning unit. That was it. The fluorescent lighting made the room feel stale.

She turned her attention back to Isaac just as he finished checking her in. He handed her a key to room 237 along with her driver's license.

"Enjoy your stay," he said.

"Thank you," she replied and looked down at her key.

"Backside," Isaac said seeing the look on her face. "And the wi-fi password is the phone number to the motel if you need to use it."

She smiled and nodded. He smiled back.

Breanna exited the office and left to find her room.

❄ ❄ ❄

When she opened the door she immediately smelled the mustiness of the room. The smell was a combination of must and bleach.

She hit the light switch and looked around. She put her bag on top of the table next to the door. It rocked. One of the legs needed to be tightened. She tried cutting on the lights on either side of the bed. Only one worked. The other didn't even have a bulb.

This damn sure ain't the Hyatt she thought to herself. No big deal though. It was cheap and she only really needed a place to lay her head at night. She could save up some money in the meantime. This would do for now.

Wanting to cleanse herself of the day, she started the shower. She turned the handle for the water to hot. Tonight she would stand under the water until her skin pruned. Stories like the one she'd heard tonight from her Damon stuck with her. Especially when they were her last or only client for the day. She needed to get the stories she heard out of her pores.

She pulled a rolled joint from her purse, sat on the toilet, and lit it. Weed would make her forget her surroundings soon enough. She could feel the steam from the shower as the bathroom began to warm up.

Breanna stepped out of the bathroom and sat down on the bed to finish smoking. The television was off, but she stared at the screen. She could see herself. A darker version. She took another drag and blew the smoke at the person on the other side of the screen.

CHAPTER 12

"How can I get a raise?"

Reggie was standing in Chris' office. It wasn't the office of a person running a Fortune 500 company; it was tucked away down a hallway no one in the building used. At the end of the hallway was a leaky water fountain that management couldn't be bothered with getting repaired.

Chris didn't have any children so pictures of his wife were all he had on his desk.

"Raise?" Chris asked.

"Yes. A raise," Reggie said looking directly into Chris' eyes. "I need more money."

"Look, Reg. You're a good worker, but we don't give raises here. We honestly can't afford to," Chris said.

"How can I make more money then?" Reggie asked.

"How many sales have you had the past few weeks?"

Chris responded with a question. Reggie hated this. It absolved the company of any responsibility for what they paid their workers. It was another way of saying it was the employees fault for not making a livable wage.

Reggie's sales had been average. It was hard to sell to a reluctant customer. Or even a customer that simply didn't need the product. Sure they'd listen to what you had to say, but they all said the same thing in the end, "No". And Reggie didn't see the point in pushing for carpet cleaning products. If they showed any interest, he'd pounce, but outside of that, it felt like a waste of time. And in the field, time was money. Next house.

"My numbers have been regular, but the end of the year is coming up. Nobody's trying to spend extra money if they don't have to. It's the holiday season. You know how this go, Chris."

They established enough of a relationship within the past year to talk straight with one another.

"I do. And I've been working at this company for 10 years now. We don't give raises Reg. That's why I push so hard all year for you guys to sell. I know what's about to happen after New Year's. Between you and me, I want your numbers to be good. All of you. I want them to be great. Honestly, that makes me look good. Listen, if you're making more money, the company is making more money and I'm making more money. But you can't cut corners. We set this up like this for you all to succeed. And succeed beyond expectations," Chris said and stared at Reggie afterward.

"I'm already a crew chief, and I don't foresee any manager positions opening up any time soon. Seems like I've hit the ceiling. I don't see how I can succeed beyond expectations when there's no upward mobility," Reggie said.

"I wouldn't say that. We've had a few cleaners come through and make some really good money. It's all about sales. That's where you make your money. Cleaning is only half the job. That upward mobility you're talking about is mastering the art of sales. It's not necessarily upward mobility within the company. It's upward mobility with your paycheck. That's what you want to increase. A position won't do that. At least not here," Chris said.

At least not here. The words repeated in Reggie's head as soon as he heard them. He could tell Chris meant what he was saying. He had hit the ceiling position-wise. But he wasn't going to quit.

Chris was still speaking as Reggie pondered ways to increase his income. Tuning back in, Reggie noticed that he'd gone into a speech he'd heard several times before.

He spoke as Chris finished his monologue, "I understand all that. But honestly, how much do you expect me to make in the next month and a half? Especially with Christmas coming up. Nobody's tryna spend a penny more than they have to. Not on their floors anyway."

"Listen, I empathize with your financial situation-"

Reggie was partially offended. Especially because Chris didn't know his financial situation. Reggie made it a point not to let anyone know about his living situation or just how bad it was for him outside of work. And it wasn't bad per se, but he lived in a motel. Most people judge you for shit like that.

"-but I can't give you any special treatment. What I'll do is give you a couple extra jobs a day. That'll help increase your chance of making a sale, but the actual selling part is up to you. I can't go against what you're saying, but I also can't take the responsibility of your paycheck out of your hands. We're responsible for your base pay. You're responsible for making anything outside of that. I hear what you're saying, but I earned my keep here by maximizing my opportunities. And I know you can too," Chris said, satisfied with himself after the remark.

Reggie was stuck for another resolution. This was the best Chris could offer and he knew it. No sense in trying for more. He would only have to listen to another lecture.

"I guess I'll have to make that work then," Reggie said.

Quitting wasn't an option. And truthfully he enjoyed the job, but anyone working for someone else will tell you that money is always the main motivation. For both the employee and employer. If you didn't know, you'd quickly be reminded by just how expendable you were at any job.

Reggie left the office to start his route.

❄ ❄ ❄

The day had been long. Reggie had managed two upsales in product. He had sold a bottle of tile and grout cleaner to a middle-aged couple looking to maintain the tile in their kitchen and master bathroom a little better in between cleanings.

He'd also sold a bottle of Red Wine Remover to an older White lady who'd become a lush since she'd retired from her position at a publishing company. He saw a dildo sitting next to her bed when he was doing the walkthrough. She spotted it too. But she was an older lady. Shame didn't register to older people in general. Their life was their life. And they weren't inviting him into their lives. They just needed things tidied up a little. They'd exchanged glances, she calmly shoved it into her nightstand, and that was that.

❄ ❄ ❄

Wearing the grime and dust from his shift, Reggie entered Reserve Gas Station. He rarely came to this station as it was across town, but decided to switch up from Smiley's. The beer was a few cents cheaper and Reggie liked to

126

glimpse the Mexican women that came in on the few occasions he had decided to make the trek.

"Aight ma. Have a good night."

The gas station employee spoke to a short Mexican woman grabbing her bag off the counter. As most foreigners do when they can't understand what you're saying, she smiled.

Both the attendant and Reggie watched her exit the store. She wore a red spaghetti strap shirt and black spandex with brown sandals. It was a little chilly for her attire, but he didn't mind. Her hips swayed as she left.

The two looked back at each other and nodded in silent understanding of the moment.

Reggie put his two tallboy Budweiser's on the counter. The attendant began ringing him up.

"And let me get a number 31 and 18," Reggie said scanning the scratch-off tickets. The attendant peeled the two tickets from the roll.

"Can I ask you something, bro?" The attendant asked putting his scan gun down.

"Sure. What's up?" Reggie said.

"You ever notice how many White homeless people be out there?" He asked pointing to the main highway beside the gas station, Yadkin Drive.

Reggie had noticed but didn't think much about it. There had always been one or two Black people mixed in the crowd.

127

The intersection was empty except for cars passing. It was late now and nobody panhandled after dark.

He nodded, "Yeah."

"You ever wonder why that is?" The attendant asked.

"No," Reggie responded dryly. He didn't consider the situations of the homeless. There were just too many of them. And everyone had their reason for living on the street. He understood people's sympathy for the homeless for religious purposes, but most of those people hadn't spent a day with a homeless person. Or had an actual conversation with them. They just looked at their efforts to help in some godly light. But Reggie knew it was all self-serving and disingenuous. Fear of the hereafter. Truthfully, if they decided to do something about homelessness and not pacify the situation things would be better off.

"Cause God is turning things around. That was supposed to be us out there. That whole crack era with Reagan. They were trying to get us all strung out and hooked on drugs. It worked for a minute. But we broke the spell. Now, look. They gotta deal with that shit now. It's they people out here strung out and homeless. Out here looking like dead folk. It says in the book of Exodus Chapter 34 Verses 6-7, "The Lord visits the iniquity of the fathers on the children and the children's children, to the third and the fourth generation." Leviticus 26:39 says,

"Because of their iniquity, and also because of the iniquities of their fathers they shall rot away like them." I saw a White boy out there today who didn't look any older than 20 holding up a sign begging for money. I'm 40, bruh. If I can work a job, I know his young White ass can find somebody that'll hire him. He on that shit man," he said.

Reggie took in the words of the attendant. More than what he said, Reggie was impressed at his ability to quote different scriptures. He could only ever remember the Golden Rule *Do unto others as you would have them do unto you* But he couldn't remember the chapter nor verse the phrase could be found in the Good Book.

The attendant continued, "They got 1000 years of suffering coming. The Bible say that. And we gonna rule over them for that 1000 years," he said.

His remark lost Reggie.

The attendant stepped back profoundly, hands raised as though he were Moses parting the Red Sea. Reggie noted this as he listened.

"Cause we the original Israelites. The Hebrews there now, they ain't the original people follow me. Black folks have been scattered. But we waking up.

A customer entered the store. An older White man. The attendant got silent and waited to see what the customer wanted. The man walked directly up to the counter and studied the lottery tickets.

Reggie watched the attendant.

"Can I have two number 29's, a 27, and a 20," the gentleman said pointing at the scratch-offs that he wanted to buy as he spoke.

The attendant rung him up and handed him his tickets.

"Have a nice day sir. Good luck," he said to the man as he exited.

"Thank you. You do the same," the man said.

The attendant waited for him to leave.

"God's gonna kill all these Crackas. Read Revelations. A lot of people scared to read it cause they scared of the truth. Black folks won't be hurt, bothered by, or even remember the White race. Cause they not gonna exist anymore. We'll forget all about them," he said.

He stared directly at Reggie as though he were waiting for him to applaud his speech.

Tired, covered in dirt, and holding two beers, and a couple of lottery tickets that might yield a profit with any luck, Reggie nodded not in agreement or understanding even. He only wanted to get to the end of the conversation.

"I hear you, man. Powerful shit you talking," Reggie said.

This pleased the attendant enough. He smiled.

"I'm telling you, brotha. We waking up," he said

"I feel you. I gotta get outta here my dude," Reggie said.

The attendant grabbed a pamphlet tucked on the side of the register and handed it to Reggie.

The 12 Tribes of Israel was printed on the front.

"Come by any Saturday man."

Reggie accepted with no plans on attending. They dapped up and Reggie left. He held the door for a mid-twenties-looking Mexican lady. He peeked at her breasts popping out of her spaghetti strap shirt, smiled, and continued on his way.

❋ ❋ ❋

Reggie was ordering tacos from his favorite taco truck.

"Two steak please," he said to the Mexican woman.

"Onions and cilantro?" She asked. As much as Reggie frequented the truck he knew she knew the answer. Her robotic response was more of a formality. *You want fries with that* he always heard in his head. Damn right he wanted fries. Every time.

"Yes. Tomatoes too," he said.

"Tomato?" She asked. He'd broken rank.

He nodded.

"7 dollar," she said.

She stood at the window and waited to be paid. During the day she'd call out the price and start cooking right away. But she was much less trusting at night. And who could blame her. A lone Mexican woman on this side of town handling cash at night could provoke the most heinous acts. But her truck was strategically parked near the camera at the corner of the building. He wasn't sure the camera worked, but at least it gave her peace of mind. Enough Mexican men walked up from time to time so Reggie figured she was covered enough.

He handed her the money and placed a dollar in the tip jar.

"Thank you," she said and smiled. "10 minutes."

Reggie nodded and turned towards Smiley's. The mini-mart stayed open until 1 to 2 a.m most nights. Chinedu's husband ran the store during the late hours.

The Mexican woman must not be married he thought to himself. *Or maybe she's just the better cook.*

A crowd of people was gathered in front of the store. Rap music was blasting from one of the cars parked in the front. It reminded Reggie of the local club back in his old neighborhood: The Lounge. Though Reggie hadn't been old enough to get in himself when he was younger, he remembered the atmosphere around his neighborhood watering hole. Loud music, people shooting pool or playing cards, men and women drinking at the bar. It always seemed like a lively place to him. There were fights, drugs, and other things. But it was a good place overall for the adults in the neighborhood to unwind after a long week.

One or two people went into the mini-mart, but everyone hung outside for the most part either conversing, drinking beer in brown paper bags, or passing a blunt on the side of the building.

132

After they finished getting drunk and high, they could meander their way over to the taco truck to satisfy the food craving that inevitably followed. Reggie suspected that this taco truck made a couple thousand dollars a day with all of the traffic.

Reggie noticed Money amongst the crowd. The life of the party because he was the dealer and had a naturally forward personality. At least when he was in the mood to entertain.

"They food any good?"

The voice came from behind Reggie. He stopped staring across the street at the mini-mart and turned to see who the voice belonged to.

Breanna stared into the window contemplating as the Mexican lady cooked Reggie's tacos. Even from her profile, Reggie noticed how pretty she was right away.

"Hell yeah. You ain't never had a taco from here?" Reggie asked.

"Obviously not. They filling?" She asked.

"Yup. She puts a lot of meat on hers."

Breanna studied the menu.

"That's usually all I get. I keep it simple. Might get something that don't agree with my stomach," he said.

Reggie makes a poor attempt at a joke. Breanna chuckled nonetheless.

"How much are they?" She asked.

"Tree-fiddy," he replied.

She pondered this for a moment while watching the Mexican lady slap two tortillas on the grill.

"How you get yours made?"

"She got 3 kinds. Pork, chicken, and steak. I've had all three but I stick with the steak. I don't know what they kill to get that meat, but it tastes amazing."

Breanna laughed out loud.

"The main two toppings are onions and cilantro. But you can add tomatoes, jalapeños, cheese, and whatever else they got in their toppings section.

As though she could hear them the Mexican lady called from the truck, "Green sauce or red sauce?"

"See what I mean?" Reggie said after he heard the question.

"Green sauce," Reggie yelled back.

She threw a small cup of green sauce in the bag, a napkin, a packet of salt and handed the bag to Reggie.

"Thank you."

She looked at Breanna. "What would you like?'

Breanna studied the menu for a moment considering whether she wanted to try a taco. "I'm good," Breanna replied waving her off.

The Mexican lady nodded, turned, and began the business of cleaning the stove.

"You missing out," Reggie said.

"I'll try it. I just wanted to check it out right now, but you make it sound like it's good."

She sniffed Reggie's bag. He folded the top over.

"It smells good too," she said.

Reggie pointed at the truck, "Well, there they are..." He motioned for her name.

She caught the hint.

"Breanna," she said.

"You gonna thank me when you get one Breanna," Reggie said.

"What's your name?" She asked.

"Reggie," he responded.

"Well, we'll see Reggie. Think I'll just grab some snacks from the store across the street tonight."

"Suit yourself," he said raising an eyebrow.

She smirked and headed across the street to Smiley's. Reggie minded her as she waited for traffic to pass before crossing. He smiled and headed to his room.

CHAPTER 13

Reggie was getting the van set up while Dustin moved all of the furniture in the rooms they'd be cleaning out of the way.

Jeremy, the customer's home whose carpet they were cleaning, was walking around his front yard inspecting it for trash. A middle-aged Black gentleman with the beginnings of gray hair. He picked up an old chip bag, thrown from the car of a passerby, out of his yard. He looked down the street as though he could materialize the chip bag culprit somehow. He shook his head and went back to tending his yard.

Reggie watched as Jeremy inspected the rest of his yard for trash or any inconsistency he may have overlooked. Reggie could tell Jeremy took pride in his home. And as he should. Reggie envisioned himself treating his yard with the same amount of

136

meticulousness. At the very least, he'd have the best floors in the neighborhood.

The other brick homes looked the same. Only the color of the shades differentiated them. All the yards were cut for the coming winter. Leaves were scattered in yards with trees. Most of the adults and kids were at work or school so the neighborhood was quiet. Winter break wasn't for another couple of weeks. The streets would be lined with kids happy to have the first half of the school year over with.

"How does it feel to have a White boy as your assistant?" Jeremy asked turning his attention to Reggie.

Though Dustin was White, Reggie hadn't thought of him in the context that Larry meant. Reggie sensed that Larry meant something more in line with slavery. Having a White assistant at a job was nothing like that. And honestly, outside of having to introduce him as his assistant, he didn't think of Dustin as his "assistant" in terms of wielding any authority over him. It was his job to make sure the cleaning got done but that was with or without Dustin being on his van. He taught him things here and there throughout the day, but other than that the main goal was learning the routine needed to complete the job day in and day out. Dustin seemed to be learning that easy enough.

He didn't feel a sense of superiority over him. Especially since the guy running the company, Chris, was White. Dustin would be promoted to crew chief after putting in his time as an assistant. That's what the system was designed for. There wasn't anywhere to go after that. Unless he stuck around for a few years and a position in management opened up. But he was antsy now. Reggie didn't see him sticking it out that long.

"Like having a Black assistant, to be honest with you. Work's gotta get done either way, but I see what you're getting at," Reggie said.

"Shiiit. Let me get a White assistant. I'd make that cracka do shit just cause. Too many White folks acting like it's the 60's or something. All these White cops killing Black men, Black women. It's spooky out here right now," Jeremy said.

Reggie laughed. He'd heard this on more than one occasion. Bigotry mostly, but he always got a good laugh out of it. It was too early in the day to kick up dust about stuff like that. But everyone felt comfortable speaking around their own so he wasn't surprised. He just wasn't going to extend the conversation any longer than he had to.

"He's a cool kid. You're not wrong in what you're saying, but we can't hold every White person responsible. Some. But that's a different story," Reggie said adding a little humor to try and change the subject or end the conversation.

"Cool or not, I'd put his ass to work if I was in your position. Cracka's at my job make me break my fucking back. If I ever get the chance..."

He trailed off as Dustin walked out of the house.

"I finished moving the furniture Reg," Dustin said from the porch.

He let the door shut behind him and lingered on the steps.

"Cool. I'll start in the back bedroom and work my way out," Reggie said.

"Aight," Dustin said and walked back into the house.

"I'm just saying, you better take advantage of your position. What color is your boss?" Jeremy asked.

"White," Reggie said.

Jeremy nodded as if Reggie's response validated his response. "See. That's exactly what I'm talking about," Jeremy said. "You out here busting your ass for some other man."

Reggie was offended. Though true, there was nothing wrong with having a job. Workers were necessary. Everybody couldn't be rich. Society wasn't meant to sustain itself in that way. Pay. That's what was more important. He couldn't say it in enough ways. Whether you were working for yourself or punching someone's clock, you wanted to make a livable wage. Needed it for real.

Jeremy was postulating.

"Like I said, I get it. I'm just trying to get my money. He does his part and I do mine," Reggie said.

Jeremy took the hint.

"Better get back to doing your part then," Jeremy said.

"I'll come get you to check the rooms when we're finished," Reggie said.

"Cool. I'll be out here," Jeremy said.

He turned and walked around the side of the house. Reggie stuck his middle finger up as soon as Jeremy rounded the corner.

Reggie started up the truck mount for the cleaning machine. The sudden burst of noise echoed through the quiet neighborhood. He grabbed the wand, slammed the side doors on the van shut and headed inside.

❄ ❄ ❄

Reggie had cleaned with no issues thus far.

Jeremy wanted the drapes in his bedroom cleaned. Dustin had brought in the upholstery tool before Reggie got in the room. He hooked it to the vacuum hose and started cleaning the drapes; making his way from the left side of the room to the right.

There were pictures of his wife and 2 daughters on top of the tallest dresser in the room. The color in the room was an Aegean blue and the flooring was White Oak hardwood.

"What do you think about the color," Dustin asked pointing to the walls.

"I wouldn't do it," Reggie said. Though he liked the color blue, he didn't care to have a whole room painted with the color. He felt that it'd make him nauseous if he stayed in the room for too long.

"Me neither," Dustin said.

The drapes weren't dirty at all. Just needed a good steam bath more than anything. Reggie ran the wand along each section and rested the bottom of the drape back on the ground. He spread them out as much as possible so they could air dry.

There wasn't much for Dustin to do as the hose didn't need to be pulled out of the room and he'd moved all of the furniture. He checked out the room while Reggie cleaned.

Aware that Jeremy was at least in earshot of his house, Dustin remained in whatever room Reggie was cleaning.

Besides the color of the walls, he did like the room. He liked the house overall. His eyes searched the room for any sign of Jeremy's occupation. He saw nothing.

There were five windows in the room so Reggie had to clean 10 drapes in all. He was cleaning the drapes for the third window.

"Fuck you doing!"

The voice made Dustin jump. Reggie, focused on cleaning the drapes and deaf to most sounds due to the sound of the vacuum hose, didn't even turn around. He tugged the wand up and down the drapes as he steamed them.

141

Dustin turned towards the door and saw Jeremy staring at him. He put up his hands as though he were caught red-handed.

"What?" he said with his hands still up.

"Fuck are you doing in this part of my bedroom?" Jeremy said as he approached.

Dustin put his hands down and froze. Jeremy got right in his face.

"I asked you what you're doing over here," Jeremy repeated.

Reggie had put down the first drape on the third window and was cleaning the second.

"Nothing. I'm waiting for Reggie to get finished so I can drag the hoses out of the room," Dustin managed to say without stuttering.

"So why ain't you standing over there next to him? What you doing over here by my dresser?" Jeremy asked and looked at his oak bureau dresser.

"I'm not doing anything. Reggie is cleaning your drapes. I'm just over here waiting for him to get done," Dustin said with more sincerity in his voice.

Jeremy was older, but he still looked like he was in good shape. Plus he could hear an extra something in his voice but couldn't make out what it was. The look in his eyes felt like more than anger.

Jeremy stared at him for a moment longer and walked over to his dresser. He opened the drawers one by one and looked inside each of them. Dustin waited until he finished.

Reggie, finished cleaning the drapes for the third window, had taken notice as he plodded over to the fourth window and came to where the two men were standing to see what was happening.

He saw the angry look on Jeremy's face immediately and hoped that things weren't going to escalate. He thought about what happened a few days prior as he walked over.

Dustin locked eyes with him and had a look of confusion. Reggie motioned for him to remain calm.

"Everything okay Jeremy?" Reggie asked as he walked up.

Jeremy took a couple of steps towards Reggie.

"I caught him over here doing something when I came in," Jeremy said.

"Doing what?" Reggie asked.

Jeremy paused. He looked around trying to find something out of place. Everything looked to be where he'd seen it the last time he was in the room.

"What up's?" Reggie asked and looked at Dustin this time.

Dustin didn't want to say anything. He just shrugged his shoulders.

Jeremy had nothing. Nothing was missing and nothing was out of place. He eyed Dustin up and down carefully.

He relented.

"How much longer before you're finished?" Jeremy asked looking at Reggie.

"About another 45 minutes with everything left to clean," Reggie said. "You need to go somewhere? You can pay before you leave if that's the case."

Reggie knew internally this wasn't an option for Jeremy. Even without him saying it, he knew that Jeremy thought Dustin had stolen something. Worse, he'd probably hoped he'd stolen something. He seemed like a bit of a live wire.

"No. I ain't got nowhere I need to be. Just wondering how much longer y'all were gonna be in my house," Jeremy said and looked at Dustin.

"Not much longer. I'm gonna finish up in here and then I'll come get you," Reggie said.

"Okay," Jeremy said and sat down in a chair in a corner of the room and stared out the window.

Reggie and Dustin looked at him and then back at each other. They shook their heads.

Hurry the fuck up Dustin mouthed.

Reggie would work as fast as he could without sacrificing quality. It seemed Jeremy was going to be joining them for the rest of the time they were cleaning.

He'd had this happen on a couple of occasions. He was normally the one being watched though. It was strange seeing it from the other side. The difference was one had caused the other, but it didn't make either necessary. But Jeremy was even above Reggie's pay level. He only saw him and Reggie as "equal" because they were Black. Financially, they couldn't be further apart.

In the grander scheme, they were fighting two different fights at the moment. Reggie judged nor faulted Jeremy for his views.

Dustin looked mostly unbothered, but Reggie could tell he wanted to leave.

He grabbed the wand and finished cleaning the drapes. Dustin stood next to him and pretended to study Reggie's cleaning technique. He could see Jeremy staring at him out the corner of his eye.

CHAPTER 14

Reggie decided to ride the metro Uptown on this chilly Saturday morning. Although he was technically on standby to be called into work, he assumed he'd be in the clear today and wanted to be around people not looking to scam a dollar. Although downtown had its share of scammers, they were less concentrated and he knew which areas to avoid.

THE NEXT STOP IS YADKIN

The feminine mechanized voice programmed into the train called out the next stop.

A few people got up from their seats, grabbing the safety bars so as not to be thrown down, anticipating the next stop.

Destitute people don't want to remain bad off the thought came to Reggie. Well, most didn't, and he surely counted himself in that number.

Constantly looking over your shoulder for fear that someone might be watching you so they could take what little you hadn't pawned to the two or three pawnshops kept in constant rotation. Unwanted conversations with winos that had let women and drink destroy their lives.

Looking around the train, he saw individuals dressed in fall attire and business casual clothes. *They don't smell like mold and bad decisions with strange bedfellows* he thought.

In a few hours, he would crawl back into the German Roach infested, moldy hell hole he'd crawled out from, but today he only wanted to enjoy some fresh air and eat at the new Soul Food spot he'd heard about on the radio while driving to one of his appointments for Fair Zone. "Annie's Kitchen." His mouth watered at the thought. The kid seated across from him caught him licking his lips and stared quizzically. Reggie made a face at him. The kid smiled and turned back to his mom and dad.

THIS STOP IS YADKIN

Reggie heard the voice as the train came to a halt. A few passengers got on, others exited.

THE DOORS ARE NOW CLOSING. PLEASE STAND BACK

Just as the doors shut, a lone college-aged woman banged on the window.

"Hey! Hey!" She yelled.

Reggie thought the train would pull off, leaving her stranded at the station but the doors opened at the last moment.

She stepped on. They locked eyes momentarily and shared a smile.

Reggie nestled into his seat. Today would be a good day he determined in his mind.

❋ ❋ ❋

How could he know the coffee shop next door to Annie's would be the stage the yet to be identified mass shooter would choose for his danse macabre. Everything up until that point had gone without a hitch. He tried a kale smoothie from one of those hippy bars popping up everywhere. He'd never had kale, but the maple syrup and banana made it go down sweet. He also ate a spicy lamb salad from one of the Halal street vendors scattered around Uptown and sat at the park for an hour. He preferred the Uptown park to the one in the neighborhood adjacent to Competitive. Sanitation aside, him being without kids and even a girlfriend, a lone Black man was less likely to look like a predator sitting all by himself there. Especially with so much life happening around the park and the occasional walk or bike through from the local police force. It made him feel funny to think he needed the police to put others at ease around him, but this was the new America. Maybe even a continuation of the old.

He'd gotten hungry again around 4 and decided to head to Annie's, maybe grab a beer or two at a Sports Bar and then head back to the motel.

The shots rang out at 4:47 pm. Approximately 32 minutes after he'd stepped foot into Annie's Kitchen and 5 minutes after he'd gotten served his plate of fried catfish, macaroni, collard greens, red beans and rice, with a Coke to wash it all down with.

Goddammit! He recalled saying aloud after the first shots were heard hours later as he smoked the blunt he left rolled for himself back at the room.

Once people were hip to the grim situation next door, panic ensued. Parents scooping up screaming children, people clamoring to get out of Annie's. Annie had saved a few lives by ushering some of her customers into the back of the restaurant and locked themselves in her office (she'd later be mentioned in the papers for this and even got interviewed on CNN; a perk that spiked business no doubt). Reggie watched a few of the customers try to get out the restauranst. He witnessed what a person looked like getting ripped apart by an AR-15. Though he wasn't a gun enthusiast, he remembered that AR stood for Armalite and not Assault Rifle as had been the common name floating around. One man had his head split down the middle with his skull showing *like a half-eaten salmon ravaged by a bear* he thought morbidly to himself. Even with his head split his body continued to run. A woman had gotten shot in the back. She hadn't died initially but died on the way to the hospital. He learned this later as he watched the news. Ten people in total were killed. Four men, three women, two children, and the gunman himself. It wasn't the cops who'd gotten the shooter. He'd put the barrel of the shotgun he carried as a second weapon into his mouth and blew his brains and skull fragments onto the pictures on the wall inside Annie's.

Reggie had escaped after seeing the woman get shot. The shooter's attention had strayed from those escaping to the few still left in the shop. Reggie had ducked around the first corner he found and was gone. Watching the news later he couldn't help but think *These are the regular people I wanted to be around to escape this shit hole? Jesus. Maybe the whole world is a shit hole. Some people just think their shit smells better. But it attracted the same flies nonetheless.* He took a drag of his blunt.

❊ ❊ ❊

Her stomach growled. A steady diet of Philly Cheesesteak subs, with imitation steak, and cheeseburgers from Smiley's had stopped filling her up after surviving on that stuff the first few days she stayed at the motel.

Goddammit," Breanna said aloud. "I'm fucking hungry."

She headed to the mini-fridge that sat in the space next to the sink. It had dents all over and if the ice built up too much on the inside, it wouldn't close causing whatever food left inside to sweat out and spoil. She had learned this on day three. She only bought cheap food to hold her over from the Dollar Store (Michael Angelo's variety packs), but she had to throw them out after they had gotten soggy. She'd chiseled the ice down and gotten the fridge to shut, but, except for drinks, she had no intentions of storing food in the fridge anymore.

Not wanting any more of Smiley's food she was stuck. *Tacos.* The thought came to her suddenly. She dug in her sweatpants pocket and pulled out a ten-dollar bill. "Fuck it," she said aloud and left the room headed for the truck.

The night air was crisp. She wore sweatpants, a jacket, and slides with socks. Smiley's parking lot was quiet. Only a few stragglers hung out at the laundromat. Except for Chinedu's husband's burgundy Expedition, there were no other cars in the lot. She saw steam rising from the taco truck as two Mexicans stood outside waiting for their orders. She walked up to the window. The Mexican lady paid her no mind as she flipped the sausages on the grill.

I usually just get the tacos she heard Reggie say in her head.

The Mexican lady peered over her shoulder and saw Breanna waiting to order.

"One minute," she yelled turning her attention back to the grill.

"Okay," Breanna said, but was sure her voice had been drowned out by the sizzle of the meat on the stove.

She observed as the woman put 4 big buns onto the grill. There was an assortment of meat. Lettuce, avocado, and all the dressings were added later.

"What's that?"

Breanna hadn't meant to ask the question aloud, but the smells were making her mouth water. It came out before she realized she was asking it.

"Cuban Sanwich," the Mexican lady replied without looking up.

"How much is it? Breanna asked.

"Ten dolla," she said.

She knew she'd try it sometime soon.

"Okay," Breanna responded.

The Mexican lady finished making the sandwiches, placed them in styrofoam to-go boxes, and handed them to the 2 Mexican men waiting outside the truck. Each requested a Coke to go with their Cuban. She gave them a glass bottle apiece, and they paid and left.

"Yes?" The Mexican lady said eyes trained on Breanna.

"Two tacos please," she responded.

"7 Dolla," she said and waited for Breanna to pay.

She handed her the ten and got three dollars back.

Hadn't those Mexican men paid after they got their food? The thought left her mind just as quickly as it had entered. Prejudice took a back seat to hunger on this night.

"Hey, pretty lady."

She turned. Money sat on his bike. His right foot was on one pedal and his left foot was on the ground. He was grinning. She could see his three gold teeth on his bottom row.

"I like your hair," he spoke again.

She gave a sarcastic smile back, "Really," she said. Her hair was in a bun. Not done up particularly nice at all. She hadn't planned on running into anyone, and, she thought to herself, *I wouldn't clean up for this mother fucker no way.*

More Roaches The thought came to her and made her chuckle aloud.

Money, oblivious, continued, "Yeah. I been seeing you around. You new here huh?"

Breanna didn't respond.

"Ah, you ain't gotta act like that. I ain't gon' bother yo cute ass. Just passing the time," Money said.

He sensed he was unwelcome. Breanna said nothing but gave him an A*lright, now what?* look.

"Well, aight then. You enjoy those tacos pretty lady," Money said.

He peddled in the direction of the street. Smiley's was really on his mind. From midnight to 4 am were prime pill selling hours. He knew which 24-hour gas stations to lurk and which dump motels the fiends hung around.

"Onions and cilantro?" The Mexican lady asked.

Her voice had broken Breanna's fixation on Money.

"Yes and tomatoes," she said.

The Mexican lady nodded.

"Green sauce or red sauce?"

"Green sauce please," she said remembering Reggie's recommendation.

She threw one cup of green sauce, a small salt packet, two limes, and a napkin into Breanna's bag and handed it to her.

"Thank you," the Mexican lady said.

"Goodnight," Breanna said.

❄ ❄ ❄

Back in her room, she unwrapped one of the tacos from the aluminum foil. She sprinkled half the salt packet onto it and then squeezed the lime over top. She poured half of the green sauce onto it after and took a big, sloppy bite.

"Mmmm hmmm," Breanna managed. She savored each bite with a smile.

He knows good food she thought as she enjoyed her tacos.

Three bites and one whole taco later she sat on the bed wiping her hands and mouth. Content. She turned on the television and caught the tail end of the local news.

"Another mass shooting," she said aloud. The tacos were catching up to her and sleep was not too far

behind. She pulled back the covers and laid down. Five
minutes later, she slept.

✳ ✳ ✳

"Get the fuck away from my door!"

Reggie snapped awake.

Money was on the other side of the door arguing
with one of his pill fiends.

"I done told y'all, man! My girl and her daughter
here! Y'all don't need to be knocking on this fucking door!
Why you ain't say shit when you seen me at the sto!?" He
yelled at the fiend.

"Sorry, my fren. I just got the money."

Reggie heard a voice say in a low tone. He could
tell the fiend was Mexican.

"Den wait til' tomorrow mutha-fucka. Or you wait
yo ass across the street!"

Reggie walked carefully to the door and peered
out of the peephole.

The Mexican was wearing blue jeans, a yellow
shirt with a gray fleece and a red baseball cap pulled low.
He stared sheepishly at Money.

"Come to this fucking door again and see what
happen. Now get the fuck from round here!" Money
yelled.

The man turned and left without another word.
Money waited for him to leave and headed back into his
room.

Reggie had heard Money shout at a few of his customers before. One or two of these fiends had knocked on his door in the wee hours of the night. He'd answered the door with pocket knife concealed in his left hand. He only had to point them next door. No need for words. As he'd learned over time, drug addicts were volatile and not to be trusted. On the off chance he would have to doll up one of their faces, he was ready.

Presently, he turned and went to his mini-fridge. Sleep wouldn't come back easily, but he knew what invitation to hand out. He grabbed a Budweiser, popped the top, and sat on the bed.

He found a rerun of Law & Order and turned up the television. He could hear Money arguing with Deborah next door; the fiend had most likely wakened her or Victoria. He sipped his beer and watched Ice-T interrogate the chosen sex offender for this episode of his favorite show.

CHAPTER 15

Monday morning. Saturday's massacre behind him (death seemed to wash over those who danced with the reaper on a daily basis), Reggie left his room and headed to work.

Breanna was standing on the railing. He saw her out of the corner of his eye and turned towards her. She sauntered over to him smiling as she did so.

"What's up?" She said as she approached.

"Nada. What's up with you Breanna?" Reggie responded.

"You can call me Bri. Hearing my full name is weird," Breanna said.

"Aight, cool. I got you. How you been Bri?" He said adding emphasis on her name.

"I've been alright. I tried those tacos you told me about the other night," she said.

"And? What'd you think?" Reggie asked with a grin.

A smile came over her face as she spoke. "You do know some good tacos. Put me right out," she said laughing.

"I told you," Reggie said. "How many you get?"

"Two, but I ate another three yesterday. I couldn't help myself."

"You better slow down. You won't shit for days you eat too many of them things."

She laughed heartily. Seeing her laugh made him smile.

Reggie, getting his first good look at her in the early morning light, noticed how much prettier she was than he'd remembered. And her laugh made her even more radiant.

"I'm just saying," Reggie said through a laugh of his own.

"They're sooo good though," she said.

"Trust me. I get it," he said.

They stared at each other for a moment.

"Where you headed off to?" She asked.

"Work," Reggie responded dryly.

"What you do?" She asked.

"I'm a carpet cleaner at Fair Zone," he said.

She nodded.

"I've heard of them. They pay pretty well?" She asked.

Reggie lifted his hand to where he's currently staying. "Hell nah. But the checks clear every two weeks so that's where I'm at with it right now. Been trying for more money, but they not trying to fork out any more dough than they have to. You know how that go," he said.

"I understand. What else you do?"

Reggie looked at her quizzically.

"Whatever they paying for. Why? You hiring?" He asked sarcastically.

She laughed. "Nope. Just wondering. Multiple incomes seem to be the new wave now," she said.

"Right. Realistically, a career would be nice. This job shit don't provide stability. At least not what I'm getting paid. But you got all these questions. What you do? How you make your money?"

Breanna didn't say anything for a moment. She looked down at her feet.

"I'm an entrepreneur," she said not looking up.

"What you sell? Bundles? Lashes?" Reggie asked only half-serious.

"No," she said.

Reggie waited for her to get into specifics or to give some kind of explanation, she remained silent. He spoke after catching the hint.

"I get it. The secretive type," he said.

She smiled playfully. "No, not at all," she responded.

"But I get the 21 questions treatment though, right? I see how it is."

"What'chu mean? It's not like that. I thought we was talking."

"I'm teasing. I won't pry." He checked his watch. "I gotta get outta here. I'll drop by when I get off if you're gonna be around later. What room you in?"

She pointed down the row towards her door. "237. I should be around. Feel free to find out," she said and smiled.

Reggie smiled back.

"See you later then Bri," he said.

"See ya."

Reggie made his way past her and down the steps. She gazed at him and then headed back to her room.

❊ ❊ ❊

"Where are you two in the house right now?" Chris asked.

Reggie had stopped cleaning and stepped outside to take the call.

"Cleaning the living room at the moment," Reggie said.

"I need you to stop what you're doing, pack up, and the both of you need to go sit in the van."

Reggie knew Chris was serious by the tone of his voice. He was suddenly focused on the conversation. He walked further into the yard away from the house and turned and stared at it.

160

"What's wrong?" Reggie asked.

"I just got a call about some missing money," Chris said.

"From who?"

"We'll figure this out. Henry and I are headed your way now. Go ahead and pack everything up and get it back in the van. Make sure Dustin is out of the house as well," Chris said in a voice much more stern than Reggie was accustomed to hearing.

Chris hung up the phone.

Reggie stared at the van. To his knowledge, nothing had been stolen.

"Shit," he said quietly to himself.

❄ ❄ ❄

Dustin, finished moving the furniture to clean underneath, stood beside the window looking out into the back yard.

"We gotta go," Reggie said as he entered the room.

He could tell his voice startled Dustin from the way his shoulders jumped.

"What do you mean?" Dustin asked. "We still got more work to do."

"I don't know yet. Chris just called and said the both of us need to pack up and sit in the van. Said he got a call about some missing money," Reggie said.

Dustin turned all the way around now.

"What the fuck?"

Reggie couldn't make out if Dustin was genuinely surprised or not from looking at him. He'd heard about assistants stealing things before so he didn't put it past him. Whatever the case, Chris and Henry would be here shortly and he would soon know what was what.

"He didn't give details, but that's what he said. He and Henry are headed this way now." Reggie glanced at the clock on the wall. "Probably won't be here for another thirty minutes," he said.

"What the fuck do we do?" Dustin asked.

"Move that furniture back as fast as you can. I'll start pulling hoses out."

"You think they'll call the cops?" Dustin asked.

Reggie stared at Dustin.

"Did you take any money?"

"Hell no," he said.

He studied Dustin for a moment trying to decipher whether he was lying. He saw nothing still.

"I doubt Chris would do that before hearing us out. I've built up enough of a rapport to get that from him. Standing here talking ain't gonna do nothing though. Where's the lady?" Reggie asked looking around.

"She's been in the guest room since she inspected her bedroom," Dustin said.

Reggie walked to the guest room and listened. He didn't hear anything. He listened a little longer and knocked with enough force to arouse her if she had fallen asleep.

Silence.

He knocked once more. Again he heard nothing.

He looked over at Dustin, "Let's get started. Chris'll reschedule this job anyways," Reggie said.

Reggie carried the cleaning wand to the van and Dustin started sliding the furniture back to its proper place. He didn't bother chipping and blocking the furniture in the areas Reggie had already cleaned.

He noticed but didn't really care if the furniture bled into the carpet.

❄ ❄ ❄

Chris and Henry pulled up fifteen minutes after they had gotten everything back into the van.

Henry was driving. Chris rode shotgun.

Chris got out and walked around to Reggie's door.

Reggie observed all of this from the mirror on the driver's side of the van.

He rolled down his window as Chris approached.

"What's up fellas?" Chris said as he looked in the van.

"You tell us," Reggie said.

"Well, apparently, the lady in the house is missing $100 from her bedroom. She says you two have been the only ones in there so she figures one of you took it," Chris said.

Both Reggie and Dustin looked at one another.

"What the fuck?" Reggie said.

"Is that true?" Chris asked ignoring Reggie's rhetorical question.

"Fuck no," Reggie responded without thinking.

Dustin shook his head no.

"Step outside," Chris said backing away from the door.

They both stepped outside. Henry, who'd gotten out of the van, stood beside Chris. He didn't speak.

"I'm gonna need the both of you to empty your pockets."

They complied. Reggie had only a cheap, clear yellow cigarette lighter and a pen. Dustin pulled rabbit ears out of his pockets.

Chris, satisfied, spoke again.

"Okay. I'm gonna go talk with her. Was she hostile towards either one of you when you did the walkthrough?" Chris asked.

"No, not at all. She seemed alright. She's been in the guest room for a while though. I even knocked before we packed up the equipment. I see now why she didn't come out," Reggie said.

"Wait here. I'll see what I can make of all of this," he responded.

Chris walked up the steps to the front door. He knocked and stepped inside.

Reggie and Dustin looked at one another and shook their heads.

"If you didn't steal anything, I wouldn't worry," Henry said finally. "These things happen. People get antsy when strangers come into their home."

"I told you they consider us strangers," Dustin snapped at Reggie.

"Yeah, well. Everybody's a stranger when money's involved," Reggie said.

"How far did you get cleaning wise?" Henry asked.

"Two rooms and a hallway," Dustin said.

"This job is gonna get rescheduled. If she wants us back that is," Henry said.

He pulled out a Maverick's red pack of cigarettes. He shook one out of the box and lit it. His first drag was a long one.

Reggie had known about cleaners being accused of theft but had never been in this position. Dustin wasn't with him so race wasn't an issue. Unless she thought he was the one who stole the money. They were in the south where older Whites were notoriously untrusting of not only Black people but minorities in general.

He looked over at Dustin. Chris had made both men empty their pockets so he was sure he hadn't stolen anything. Dustin wasn't jittery and showed no signs of nerves.

Henry kept his eyes on the door. The smell of his cigarette made Reggie want one, but he didn't care for reds. *Might as well quit smoking* he felt if that was your cigarette of choice.

The three men waited in silence.

❄ ❄ ❄

Chris walked out just as Henry was finishing his cigarette.

"She forgot she put the money in a different purse," Chris said as he approached.

Reggie threw up his hands. Both Henry and Dustin laughed.

"Really?" Dustin said.

"That's the way it goes sometimes. But the important thing is she found her money and it wasn't in either of your pockets. Honestly, she's a little red at the moment, so I told her we'd reschedule for tomorrow. I'll send a different crew so it isn't awkward for anybody," Chris said.

"What do we do now?" Reggie asked.

Chris looked at his watch. It was 12:35 pm.

"Go to lunch. I'll send you your next job when we're back at the Route Room." Chris pulled $40 out of his pocket. "She asked that I give this to you to make up for the accusation. Lunch is on her today," Chris said holding a $20 bill for each of them.

Reggie felt a way about the accusation, but free money was free money. And they didn't even have to finish cleaning. Fair enough. They both took the money.

"Sorry about this guys. Homeowners are interesting people. Stick around in this business long enough and you'll learn that. I wouldn't let this bother you. It's water under the bridge now. You two still got your heads in the game, right?" Chris asked.

"Yeah, I'm straight," Reggie responded.

"I'm fine," Dustin said.

"Good. Now go enjoy your lunch," Chris said and walked back to the van.

Henry nodded to both Reggie and Dustin and followed Chris. He climbed into the driver's side, turned the van on, and backed out of the driveway.

Reggie and Dustin waited until they were out of sight before climbing back into the van. They left after.

❋ ❋ ❋

Freshly showered, Reggie went down to the taco truck and ordered two Cuban sandwiches.

"No pineapples please," he said to the Mexican lady after he ordered.

"10 minutes," she responded.

Reggie nodded and went across the street to Smiley's. He bought a six-pack of Corona beer, two bottled waters and left.

He liked when Chinedu's husband ran the store. He was far less chatty. He only asked "How are you" as a pleasantry and then told you the total for your items. In and out.

He took the beer and water to the taco stand and waited for the food to finish.

❋ ❋ ❋

167

237. He arrived in front of Breanna's door with food and beverages in hand. He knocked and heard feet shuffle inside the room.

"Hey!" Breanna beamed as she opened the door.

"Hope you haven't had dinner yet," Reggie said holding up the food and beer.

"Jeez," Breanna said surprised. "No, I haven't."

She stepped to the side and Reggie entered.

❀ ❀ ❀

Two beers deep apiece with half a Cuban left for Breanna and an empty styrofoam container for Reggie, they sat on the bed and talked. Reggie pried once more about her being an "entrepreneur" but was quickly shut down. He decided it best to let sleeping dogs lie and didn't bother prying further. She'd come around if and when she wanted to. It'd been some time since he'd sat with a woman. He tried his luck once when he'd first moved in the motel, but a lot of the women had poor hygiene, and he always felt unshakably that they'd rob him blind if given the chance. It was a feeling hard to articulate, but he felt, that wasn't right, he knew that a woman with close to nothing going for herself was a leech. And once they sunk their teeth in by chance or by dance they'd bleed you dry and move on to the next poor sap foolish enough to take them in.

"Damn. But at least she gave you both $20 to apologize," Breanna said buzzed from the Corona.

Reggie could tell she didn't drink very often.

168

"I guess so. It didn't bother me though. Just annoying," Reggie said. "You see what happened Uptown Saturday on the news?"

"Yeah, that crazy White boy shot all those people. I was falling asleep when I saw the story. That shit seems to be happening a lot nowadays," Breanna said.

"I was there," Reggie said.

Breanna's eyes widened. "You were there? Like in the coffee shop?"

Reggie cracked open his third Corona. "Nah, not in the coffee shop. I was next door at Annie's Kitchen. Heard when the shots started ringing out and the roaches started scattering."

Breanna laughed. "It's not funny, but the way you said roaches started scattering is funny." She got serious again. "You see any of the bodies?"

As sure as people slowing down to look at car accidents, Reggie knew this question was coming. Common curiosity about morbid things. He could see the look of genuine interest in her face

"I saw the moment the man and woman who ran out of the shop got murdered. Watched his head split open like a woman giving birth. The woman didn't die til' later, but I saw her collapse after getting shot in the back," he said.

Breanna stared in shock.

"Oh. My. God. Did he.. Did he die instantly?"

Reggie never thought of the question. Just figured he had. But he did recall the brain remaining active after death. Or, in this case, what was left of the poor guy's brain on either side of his head.

"I sure hope so," is all he could think to say.

Breanna shook her head, "People are scary."

Baby girl. Do you know what side of town you on? He thought to himself. "Yeah," he said and took a swig of beer.

"You give a statement to the cops?"

"Nah. I dipped out. Didn't see his face anyway. Found out later that the guy killed himself so there isn't a need for a statement now. Shit. I still don't understand why people do that."

"Do what?" She asked.

"Kill a bunch of innocent people and then turn the gun on themself. Why not start with yourself?" He chuckled. "Hell, if you survive that you've earned the right to kill. Have at it. All those funerals and lives lost just for a muh-fucka to prove a point or get famous. I don't know. What I do know, and the gunslingers of today's metropolitans don't realize, is that with this 24-hour news cycle they're just a drop in the ocean. A wave that breaks up the usual gloom and doom only to crash on the beach. They're just waiting for the next wave."

Reggie sipped his beer.

"Are you some kinda poet?"

Reggie stopped drinking. "What?"

"That was very poetic. Sad, but beautiful at the same time," Breanna said.

"Nah. Just the way it is. Can I use your bathroom?" He asked.

"It's right where it is in your room," Breanna said pointing in the direction.

Reggie got up, headed to the bathroom, and shut the door behind him.

Breanna popped the top on the last Corona and took a big gulp.

The toilet flushed. Reggie exited the bathroom and sat down on the bed. Breanna sat down next to him.

Reggie turned to her, "You ever watch-"

She kissed him deeply. Passionately. Reggie was surprised but didn't resist.

She came three times before he finished. Reggie had never made love so the thought of making love never entered his mind, but he thoroughly enjoyed the sex. As a man's mind tended to do when he's troubled, his thoughts drifted to his finances and what he could do to leave Competitive, but he pushed them aside once things got going. Hearing her moans helped quiet those demons. Reggie was asleep not long after climaxing. Breanna had gotten up to pee, but she fell asleep as soon as she climbed back into bed.

CHAPTER 16

The scooter he'd seen a few weeks ago was parked in a spot at Competitive. Reggie had only seen the scooter though. Dale (the presumed name of the owner of the scooter judging from the license plate) was nowhere in sight.

He couldn't make out the color the last time he'd seen it because it had been late at night, but seeing it now in the light he was able to get a good look at it. The color was dark blue with orange flames. Reggie had seen a few scooters around the city and could tell this was one of the gas powered ones. He maintained his distance in case Dale decided to pop out of his room. Reggie studied the rooms briefly. No one was outside nor was anyone peaking out of their window.

"You got a cigarette blood?"

Derrick Jones, 6'5" in stature but his gut hung over his belt. A tall and chubby kid of about 19 years old. His face, dusty-looking, carried the eyes of someone who had seen a lot in his young existence. Probably did a lot of things too. The type of kid who was able to throw his weight around in High School. Maybe bully a few kids but got his way eventually one way or another. Might've even banged one of his young female teachers (cause 24-year-old teachers were in heat across the country apparently) but the world, the real world, was eating him alive. Little to no education, if he did graduate, and no trade to speak of. Derrick was left to fend for himself.

Reggie saw him around the motel every few weeks. He left when his money ran out but always came back after he hustled enough to pay for another week. Bus passes, metro cards, clothes; he hustled everything. If he could touch it, he could sell it.

Standing in the parking lot at Competitive, Reggie felt empathy for the young man. Probably for the first time since bumping into him. Men, young or old, couldn't survive in that lifestyle. It was only a matter of time before desperation set in and the antes for what one would do to survive were raised.

"I sure don't, bruh," Reggie said.

"You got a blunt to smoke?" Derrick asked.

He did. "Nah," Reggie said.

"I'll trade you a metro card for a blunt of loud," Derrick said in a last attempt to barter for weed.

Reggie didn't care that the kid smoked weed. He might've even smoked him out under different circumstances. But he didn't feel right giving the kid weed. You wanna smoke? Find it and buy it yourself.

"I ain't got it, my dude," Reggie said.

Derrick gave him a once over scanning him from top to bottom. He didn't say anything, just nodded his head in recognition of defeat.

Reggie reached in his pocket, pulled out $10.

"Here, bruh," he said and handed the money to Derrick.

"Aight, bet big bruh. Good looks," Derrick said. A half-smile replaced the serial killer look on his face.

It wasn't any of Reggie's business what he did with the money. That was between him and Uncle Sam.

❄ ❄ ❄

The employees lingered in the office after the morning meeting. Chris finished eating a chocolate donut from one of the boxes that sat next to him on a desk. He brought two dozen for the meeting.

Reggie and Dustin stood in the back of the room closest to the exit talking.

"You check the route for today yet?" Dustin asked.

"Yeah. I checked it. We got a light day. Five stops unless they add more. Three of those are only getting the minimum amount cleaned. Two rooms and a hall," Reggie said.

174

"Cool. I'm not in the mood to do too much today," Dustin said.

"Everything good?" Reggie asked.

"Nah, but whatever. I'm tired more than anything," Dustin said.

"Shut yo' young ass up," Reggie joked.

Dustin smiled and laughed a little. Reggie had an idea of what Dustin meant. Physically, he could tell Dustin was in good shape just by looking at him. If he didn't get an office job in about 20 years he'd probably have the limp he'd seen a lot of men develop from years of manual labor. Back problems and knee pains. But for now, he was still in good shape. What was happening to him was mental exhaustion. His girl was pregnant and he didn't have much of a way to provide for the three of them. Probably was struggling with just the two of them. He had noticed a little change but hadn't mentioned anything. But he saw the look in Dustin's eyes. His mind was spent.

"You know what I mean," Dustin said.

"I get it, man. But we don't have much to do today so don't even worry about it," Reggie said.

Larry burst through the exit and slid between Dustin and Reggie. He made a beeline towards one of the employees.

Chris and Henry froze in shock. Everyone else in the room waited for whatever was about to unfold to play out.

Larry walked up to Jason Wallace. He and Larry were about the same age. He'd been at Fair Zone three years. From what Reggie had heard, he didn't have a GED nor did he care to get one.

Reggie rode on Jason's van as an assistant a few times when he first started at the company, but they weren't friends. They'd give the occasional head nod in acknowledgment of one another but never carried a conversation after Reggie had stopped being his assistant. He did see him and Larry standing together often at the shop. He was sure Larry was selling him vape pens and weed but he smoked him out a lot of times before leaving the shop in the morning. Only with the vape pens though. Chris even smoked a vape pen. He liked the flavored tobacco. From what he said, he'd stopped smoking weed once he graduated college. But he never paid attention to Larry or any of the other guys with the vape pens. He just assumed they all smoked e-cigarettes and never questioned what liquid they used.

Larry grabbed Jason as though he were wearing lapels.

"Where the fuck is my bookbag?" Larry demanded.

Larry didn't shout. It sounded as though he were almost grinding his teeth as he spoke.

"What?" Jason asked confused.

Larry shook him violently. Jason's head resembled a new born's loose neck as he swayed in Larry's grip.

"My bag motherfucker. Where is it?" Larry asked.

Chris started towards the two men. No one else in the room made a move to break up the situation.

"Hey!" Chris shouted as he regained his nerve.

Larry punched Jason in the face. He went over a few desks in the room. The technicians let out an "oooooh" in unison.

Chris grabbed Larry by his arms and pulled him back.

Larry didn't say anything. He didn't even resist. He watched Jason gather himself.

"What the fuck is your problem!" Jason shouted and turned. He was still disoriented and swayed on his feet.

Reggie knew the bookbag Larry was talking about. It was the one he kept his weed products in. He brought it to work and kept it in his van in the morning. He made early morning sales at the shop if any of the techs needed anything, but no one bothered his bag. They all knew where he kept it though. If Jason had taken the bag, getting punched in the face might have been the least of what he'd need to be worried about.

"Walk outside and cool off," Chris said to Larry as he released him.

Larry glared at Jason, turned, and left the room.

"The rest of you head to your vans and get your routes started. Come on, guys!" He looked at Jason.

"Come with me," Chris said and walked Jason out of the room.

"Oh shit," Dustin said once Chris and Jason had left.

Reggie only shook his head.

"You think he took it?" Dustin asked.

"His bookbag?" Reggie shrugged. "I don't know. That's none of my business man."

"You right. Fucked up if he did though," Dustin said.

Reggie nodded. They could both agree on that point.

❄ ❄ ❄

Back at Competitive, Reggie was standing outside. He preferred to smoke inside, but he wasn't in the mood to sit in his room so he made an exception for tonight.

He saw a single light bend the corner of the motel as he smoked. It was dark, but he made out the orange flame as the scooter passed through the light from the lamp post that lined the fence adjacent to the motel. It was Dale. Or whatever the man's name may be.

Reggie smoked and observed as he parked the scooter. The rider gathered himself and grabbed some items out of the small trunk attached to the back of his scooter.

Reggie saw Derrick approach Dale before he noticed because of his vantage point.

178

Reggie saw he was carrying something and squinted to try and make out what it was. When Derrick grabbed it with both hands, Reggie saw that it was a shoebox. He couldn't make out the brand. It was a crapshoot on whether or not they'd even be the right size but he immediately knew why Derrick was approaching. There was no reason to try and sell shoes this late at night, but money didn't sleep and Derrick wouldn't be sleeping at the motel much longer if he couldn't hustle up enough to pay for his stay.

Dale turned when he felt Derrick approaching.

Derrick held out the box as he got closer.

"You need shoes, big bro?" Derrick said and slowed his stride as he got closer.

Dale looked down and waved him off immediately.

"You ain't even checked em' out yet," Derrick said opening the box. "These shits fresh. I'll give you a good price for em' too," Derrick said.

"I'm good bro," Dale said.

Reggie saw Derrick look around for a moment and then back to Dale. Reggie had seen that enough to know what was coming next, but apparently, Dale had too.

Derrick turned back around and had pulled his fist back with every intention to catch Dale with a sucker punch.

179

If he hadn't turned around, he would have seen Dale pull the .45 automatic pistol from his waist.

Derrick was dead before he hit the pavement.

Reggie stepped back into the shadows. Heading into his room would draw attention to himself.

Dale hopped on his scooter and pulled off. Blood started to pool around Derrick's body. Reggie stood still waiting. There was silence and then he heard the doors of the few people staying at the motel begin to open. A woman screamed downstairs.

Praise Dale-Raise Hell

❄ ❄ ❄

"What happened big bruh?"

It was the next morning. Reggie had bumped into Money as he left his room headed for work. Money was drinking a beer.

"I don't know," Reggie said. "I know that kid that stays here every few weeks is dead now."

Reggie didn't want to tell Money that he had seen what happened. Not that it mattered. Money was crooked himself. Who was he going to tell? But Reggie would be taking that information to the grave.

"Yeah. Derrick. That was my patna. I looked out for him when I could. He wasn't wrapped too tight, but he was aight. Life fucked him up," Money said.

Reggie hadn't realized that Money had known Derrick. Or at least knew enough about him and his situation to look out for him.

Money shrugged his shoulders. "What could you do big bruh? Look out for yourself at the end of the day. Shit happens too fast," Money said and downed the rest of the beer he'd been holding. "These niggas die too young. They ain't even gettin' old enough to realize the shit they willing to die fo' don't mean a damn thang," he burped. "They lives only good for the worms."

Reggie shuddered when he thought about how fast Derrick had gone from the land of the living to the realm of the dead.

"Too fast," Money repeated and burped again. "You headed to work?" Money asked looking Reggie up and down.

"Yeah. Bout to go punch this clock," Reggie said.

"Stay up then big bruh," Money said and extended his fist.

Reggie gave him a fist bump and left.

181

CHAPTER 17

Hangman Inn. Though you wouldn't know it from the name, it was a decent hotel on a decent side of town. Wooden floors, no roaches, no rust on the mini-fridge, and no mini-fridge at all for that matter. The room included a full-size refrigerator and a kitchenette. And no lingering mold from years of water damage.

Breanna lay on the bed in room 407. She was wearing black leather lingerie. She took a swallow from a mini bottle of vodka and absentmindedly flipped through the channels while she waited for her Damon.

As she waited, her thoughts drifted to her time on the streets. She didn't miss working the stroll or how dangerous that lifestyle was, but she couldn't control the memories nor when they decided to flow from her subconscious.

She'd taken a liking to one girl. They had run the streets for two years together. Breanna showed her the ropes. How to survive on the streets. What John's to ignore and which ones needed a kick in the ass. Maggie had been her name. Or least the name she'd given Breanna. Bonnie was the name she'd given Maggie to call her. Maggie's John's called her "Mags". Maggie told Breanna a client said he enjoyed putting her on his dick in a poor attempt at a condom joke. She laughed it off, but put a sexier spin on the joke and used it as a line for her clients.

Breanna hardly loved anyone, so it wasn't love, but through force of circumstances, the two women grew close over time. A young White female with a pretty face, small tits, and a good ass. She started making money her first day on the stroll. When she and Breanna linked up, they had been requested in pairs on several occasions. They mostly turned down the request but had obliged a time or two. Only when the money was worth it.

That was last year. Maggie had decided to work alone one night. Breanna had taken the night off. She did this from time to time, but Maggie was young and ambitious. *Scared money don't make money baby girl* She'd say when Breanna took a break. Maggie had worked the stroll by herself a dozen times so Breanna didn't argue with her. They took some shots of vodka and Maggie left for the night.

183

That was the last night Breanna saw her friend. The media didn't run reports for missing hookers so her disappearance was never reported on the local news. No reporters came questioning, no missing person flyers, no tweets, no Facebook post, nothing. Another girl lost. Breanna checked at the places they'd usually meet up. She went back to those spots for a few days. Nothing. It pained her not to know if Maggie was alive, but out on the streets, she assumed the worst. After a couple of weeks, she moved on. But she never took to another Maggie.

Knock-Knock

The sound of the knocking snapped Breanna out of her daze. She downed the rest of the Vodka and prepped herself.

Please don't let him be old the thought ran through her mind as she opened the door.

He was old. Not ancient. Mid-sixties she guessed. White with salt and pepper hair. A learned man in a suit, but a desperate man in facial expression. Breanna put on her best smile and seductively invited him in. *Scared money don't make money baby girl* she thought.

"I've been bad Missy. I need a spanking," the man said as he crossed into the room.

"Missy got your medicine," Breanna said as she closed the door.

❄ ❄ ❄

Breanna clutched her food as she made her way down the sidewalk headed back to Competitive. Though the trains ran late, the bus stopped running after 10 pm.

No one else had gotten off at her stop. She was glad not to have had to walk back with anyone. The silence would only make for unnecessary awkwardness. And worse if it were a man. The night turned even normal men into something else at times.

"Hey, pretty lady."

Even though the voice came from behind her, she recognized it instantly. It was Money. They'd had no formal introduction (and she'd hoped to avoid one altogether), but she knew he lived next door to Reggie. She saw him outside either tinkering with his bike, drinking or smoking and made a point to avoid coming out of the room unless it was necessary when he was.

Money, riding his bike, pedaled around her.

"I know you hear me," Money said as he parked his bike in front of her.

Breanna saw that her path was blocked and was more annoyed than scared. He seemed off, but she'd dealt with different men. Money seemed more childish than dangerous.

"What you want?" Breanna asked.

"I want you," Money said.

"What you want me for? Don't you got an old lady?" Breanna said. She'd seen the woman staying with Money a few times. She'd had a young girl with her every time. They kept to themselves though and never hung around the motel.

"Don't worry about all that. I'm talking bout you right now," Money said.

"And you ain't talking bout much. I'm not interested, it's late and I'd like to get back to the room," Breanna said.

Money laughed. This only annoyed Breanna more. He was intent on wasting her time. She'd almost wished someone had gotten off at the stop with her. She'd probably have been able to avoid the encounter she currently found herself in.

"Don't act like that. I see you and Reggie got something going on. I got my old lady too. You know that. I ain't trying to mess nothing up y'all got going on either. I just want my turn," Money said.

Breanna was disgusted. She didn't feel that his statement deserved a response and made a half-attempt to push past him. Money didn't budge.

"What's wrong? My money ain't no good?" Money said.

She didn't have mace, a knife, or a weapon of any kind. She decided to oblige him for a moment. If only to speed the interaction along.

"What's your name?" Breanna asked.

"Money," he said with a smile.

Breanna looked him up and down.

"What?" She asked confused.

Breanna wasn't sure what she thought his name was, but that wasn't what she was expecting to hear.

"That's what they call me out here. That's my name. Money. What's yo' name, pretty lady?"

"Bonnie," Breanna said.

She wasn't going to be sleeping with Money, but he'd get the name that the men with all the pent-up energy got.

"Bonnie? You shittin' me?" Money asked rhetorically.

"Bonnie," Breanna repeated.

"Let me be yo Clyde then," Money said and smiled as if he thought that was the first time she'd heard that line.

"Really?" Breanna asked rhetorically.

Money was oblivious to her sarcasm. He was in his own head. He didn't care if she was being sarcastic or not. He was getting somewhere in his mind.

"I'd like to try," Money said.

"I bet you would," Breanna said and laughed.

Money's smile turned to a look of anger. He stared at her.

"What the fuck is so fucking funny?" He asked.

"Calm down. What you got to be so mad about?" Breanna said.

The look in her eyes made Money calm down. Pretty women had that effect on men.

"I'm flattered and all, but I'm going back to my room and you're going to wherever you're going. This ain't happening," Breanna said.

She didn't know where he was headed, but he hadn't been out stalking her. He must have seen her get off the train and decided to stop. She wasn't his target.

"I understand. But I don't mind making myself known," Money said.

She nodded but didn't say anything.

Money walked his bike backward, unblocking her path down the sidewalk.

"You be safe out here Bonnie," Money said and pedaled off in the opposite direction.

Breanna only watched long enough to make sure he wouldn't decide to double back. She'd met the Devil on a lonesome night and survived. She quickened her pace back to the motel.

❊ ❊ ❊

She held her head under the showerhead and let the water run down her back and watched as the water ran down the drain.

The day had been long and she was grateful to be done with it. The lukewarm water felt good. It always relaxed her after a night with Damon.

She took the time in the shower to regain her focus. And her reasons for staying with the lifestyle. Money.

Not the roach scurrying around Competitive Inn she thought to herself.

With an end game in mind, she was able to maintain her sanity.

She hadn't needed to cut into her savings to afford her stay at Competitive. It was cheap considering prices at other motels.

She replayed thoughts in her head of Damon, John, and Maggie. The thoughts eventually swirled into an abstract portrait of chaos in her mind. She threw her head back in the shower and stared at the wall.

She thought of Reggie. She was still unsure of his intentions, but he didn't come across like the men in her profession. There was something about him that she couldn't figure out though. His eyes seemed sad to her. Longing even. But she wouldn't pry. There were still questions he wanted her to answer so she wouldn't force her own.

He'd been the first man she'd had sex with since she'd stopped sleeping with her Johns. She didn't trust him, but she would see where things went. At the very least, she enjoyed the company of a man that didn't need to be controlled nor use her for his hatred of the world. Reggie had been gentle.

She turned off the shower and grabbed a towel from the towel bar on the wall to dry off.

❊ ❊ ❊

"Let me know if you need help finding anything," the store manager of the Family Dollar said to Breanna as she walked into the store.

Breanna stopped by the Family Dollar to pick up a few items. She arrived early enough that they were still setting up for the day. The cashier and store manager were dragging u-boats of water that they kept in front of the store outside and also a few items that were on sale were being put on a table near the register.

"Okay, I will. Thanks," Breanna said.

An older Black woman perused the aisles. Early morning errands were a trend for the elderly, but Breanna found it as good practice. She could get what she needed and get back to her room. This avoided the rush of people and long lines.

She needed a few feminine items and she wanted snacks for the room. All small things. She wasn't looking to take too much on the bus ride back.

A White female with purple hair walked in. Breanna noticed her immediately. The woman glanced at Breanna but didn't stare.

Breanna recognized her from her time working the stroll. She was a prostitute. Meth had been her drug of choice and from the red spots and sunken look of her face, it still was.

She wasn't looking to hold a conversation, she only wanted her items. She made her way to the aisle with the feminine products. Breanna browsed the

190

tampons looking for which she needed. Her period hadn't started, but she was getting cramps. That was her signal that things were going to get real.

"What is you doing back in my store!"

Breanna heard the store manager yell out and knew immediately who she was talking to.

Breanna walked down the aisle as she heard the response.

The two women squared off in front of the wine bottle display. Breanna paused at the head of the aisle and peered at the two ladies.

"Girl, what?"

"I told you not to come back in here. You don't do nothing but steal!" The store manager gesticulated as she yelled.

The older Black woman was standing at the register waiting on the cashier who was frozen at the front door.

"Get out!" The store manager yelled.

"I ain't gotta go nowhere. My money good here just like everybody else," the prostitute said.

She covered her mouth as she spoke. Breanna remembered what her meth teeth looked like. She was right to hide them.

"I said get out!"

"Bitch-"

Breanna knew instantly that was the trigger word.

"I got yo bitch!" the store manager said and grabbed a bottle of Pink Moscato.

"If you hit me with that, I'll fucking kill you bitch," the prostitute said.

A standoff at high noon. Neither of the women gave ground.

"Don't lose yo' job over her," the older Black woman chimed in at the register. "Just call the police."

The store manager put the bottle down.

"Yeah, that's what the fuck I thought," the prostitute said.

"Look. You might as well leave cause ain't nobody ringing you up. And if you play with me today I will call the police. Just take yo' dusty ass back to that little strip you be working you rat bitch," the store manager said.

There was silence for a moment.

The prostitute had a lot of bark, but she wasn't going to fight. She looked around. Everyone was staring at her. She dropped the handcart she was holding and left the store.

"Thank you mother," the store manager said to the older Black woman.

She wasn't her mother, but it was a common reference for older Black women in the south.

"You're fine. I know you got a lot on yo' hands running this store baby," the woman said.

The cashier walked behind the register and started ringing up the woman's items.

Breanna went back down the aisle and finished shopping.

CHAPTER 18

Headed back to his room from Smiley's, Reggie spotted Crock Pot Man talking with another gentleman outside of one of the rooms at the motel. Reggie could tell they were haggling over the price of the crockpot.

A woman poked her head out of the door while the two men conversed and listened to the interaction. He figured she was either on the clock or the girlfriend of the man who was staying in the room.

Reggie heard children playing in the room as he approached.

The man pulled $10 from his pocket and handed it to Crock Pot Man. Crock Pot Man handed the man his newly purchased crockpot afterward.

He handed it to his girlfriend and she quickly turned and disappeared into the room.

Crock Pot Man, satisfied with himself, turned and walked in Reggie's direction and nodded his head as he passed. Reggie nodded and continued walking to his room.

Pest aside, being able to cook a meal, especially with kids in the room, was a money saver. Fast food was expensive seven days a week. Considering they were going to be staying awhile, it was in their best interest to cook meals that would last.

❊ ❊ ❊

"Please. All I ask is that you be mindful of my cats."

Reggie was solo today. Chris put Dustin on Larry's van so he could help him clean a church that had recently signed up for Fair Zone's services. It wasn't a Mega Church, but it was still pretty big. It'd take one man 8 hours to clean Chris had said. Having one more person might not cut the time in half exactly, but it wouldn't take all day either. And bigger jobs meant higher commissions so Dustin jumped at the chance.

Chris made sure Reggie's route wasn't anything too extensive.

He stood in the living room of Bethany Anderson. Old and blind (as she admitted to Reggie when she was letting him in though he could tell by the foggy look in her left eye), she had been a cat woman for some years it seemed.

The once white carpet in the living room was now badly stained and smelled awful.

Looking around the living room, Reggie could see one cat sitting on top of the coffee table. Another was lying on the back of the sofa and another sat on the window sill. Three in total, but he couldn't imagine just three cats having that bad a smell. That or she hadn't cleaned up after them in years.

"How many do you have?" Reggie asked focusing his attention back on Bethany.

"10," Bethany said.

Reggie didn't mean to look shocked, but he couldn't help it. He looked around trying to see if there were more lurking around.

"They're my babies. I used to run a rescue home, but I got too old to keep taking them in. I gave a few away and kept everyone else. You may see my orange and black cat around. He can't see for shit none either. And he's mostly deaf too so there's that. You may have to scoot him out of your way. Most of em' will probably hide or run from the sound of the wand while you're cleaning so they shouldn't be a bother. Just come and get me if you need anything," Bethany said.

"Okay. I don't think they'll be an issue," Reggie said.

Bethany nodded.

"You think that smell will be gone when you're done?" she asked.

He could tell urine and probably shit had marinated into the carpet. Even with the deodorizer the smell wouldn't be gone. What she needed was a new carpet altogether.

"How old is the carpet?" Reggie asked.

"Been here 40 years and this is the original carpet," Bethany said.

"How often do you get it cleaned?" He inquired further.

"Not too often. I use to have you guys come out for me when I needed it cleaned regularly, but things got tight. After my bills I gotta use the rest for groceries and my medication," Bethany said.

Reggie picked up on what she was saying.

"I'll put a little more elbow grease into the carpet and go heavy with the deodorizer. It won't go away completely, but it'll be better," Reggie said. "The weather's been on and off. If you're up for it and we get a warm day soon, I'd open a window or two and air the house out," Reggie said.

"I'd need to put all the cats in one room," Bethany said to herself. "How long should I keep the windows open?" Bethany asked.

"A couple hours. Not long. Just to cycle some fresh air into the house. It's a good habit with all the cats you got around here," Reggie said.

"Okay. I'll check and see what the weather's doing later this week then. I'll go ahead and get out your way," Bethany said and went into the kitchen after.

Reggie headed to the bedroom to start cleaning.

❋ ❋ ❋

Bethany sat at the kitchen table while Reggie was cleaning. She had the television on and was listening to one of the afternoon court shows.

Reggie had cleaned his way into the living room. Bethany was right about the cats running away. He hadn't seen a single one while he'd been cleaning the rooms. He was relieved by this because he didn't care to "scoot" any of the cats out of the way. Cats seemed never to forget and were constantly plotting on their owners. And he just didn't care to be attacked by some old woman's cats.

He had seen the orange and black cat sitting at the top of the steps. It had given Reggie the creeps. Blind and deaf, he'd sat there at the top watching Reggie as he climbed the steps. Reggie wasn't even sure if he could see him or not. The cat only turned his head once Reggie had walked past. He figured that was its favorite spot and would probably sit there for hours. Still, both of the cats' eyes resembled the foggy look in Bethany's left eye.

A witch and her cats Reggie thought as he climbed the steps with the steam line

He was careful not to knock the cat down the steps with his vacuum hose. The cat sat there the entire time he was upstairs and even as he drug the vacuum hose back downstairs. He made sure not to look at it on his way down the steps.

198

Reggie knew he would need to move the sofa in the living room to clean underneath. It wasn't large and he didn't mind the task. He lifted one side, slid it forward, and went to the other side to do the same.

When he lifted the sofa he saw two dead cats underneath. He dropped the chair and looked over at the kitchen. He could still hear the court show going on. Bethany hadn't moved.

He looked down at the cats. They looked to have been dead for some time. He was surprised Bethany wasn't dead. A combination of urine, feces, and dead cat scent in the air should have been a hazardous combination.

He felt bad and considered not telling her. She'd surely mourn the loss of her cats. Maybe even blame him somehow. That seemed to be a theme with customers.

Against his better judgment, he went to grab Bethany from the kitchen and brought her into the living room. He pointed out the two bodies of the dead cats.

He'd never heard a woman scream that loud and he'd never forget how it sounded for the remainder of his time at Fair Zone. She didn't faint as he thought she might though.

He offered to help her clean up the cats, but she denied his help. She put them in a black garbage bag and walked them to the garage.

Reggie finished cleaning the carpet and treating it with deodorizer and left soon after.

Bethany left the check on the counter and was in the garage for the remainder of the time he was in the house.

It had been a terrible way to end a slow day. He didn't bother her. He slid the couch back into place after he sprayed deodorizer, closed the door, and locked it behind himself when he left.

※ ※ ※

With a ticket and a beer, Reggie sat and drank. He'd stood in the shower for almost an hour just to make sure he'd gotten the smell of dead cat and piss off of him.

He'd even thought of that damned creepy orange and white cat once or twice. He hoped it didn't haunt his dreams.

Reggie was halfway through the beer and staring at the lottery ticket.

His old friend. This wasn't the last couple of dollars, but he wanted to win nonetheless.

The television was off. He sat on the edge of the bed reading the back of the ticket for play instructions as though it weren't just a matching game he'd played numerous times.

APPROXIMATE OVERALL ODDS INCLUDING BREAKEVEN PRIZES ARE 1:4.76

He read the odds of winning. He just needed to be the 1 tonight. He wanted the grand prize. Just to be done with his problems. The $200,000 prize ($139,000 after taxes). He'd take the lump sum and be gone.

He drank and stared at the ticket longer.

There were no roaches in the room. Or at least he didn't see any currently. He could hear the television next door in Money's room. Deborah and Victoria were probably alone in the room. It was usually quietest when it was just the two of them.

It was just him and the four walls. The room still felt muggy from the shower. The window in the main area was fogged.

Reggie stared at his reflection on the television. He saw himself staring back at him. Just a man. A man trying to climb out of mediocrity and a shitty dead-end job.

And he hoped he'd be $200,000 richer after he scratched a few numbers.

He finished up the beer and grabbed another from the mini-fridge. He popped the top and picked the ticket back up. He flipped it and studied the back again. No new words had appeared.

Reggie grabbed a dime off of the desk and revealed the winning numbers: 12, 8, 4, 10. He was a little shocked at the numbers. He'd never gotten a ticket with all low numbers. At least not when he played $5 tickets.

He started scratching the numbers looking for a match. He matched the 12 and won $10. Not exactly a home run, but he'd doubled up. He sipped his beer and stared at the $10 win. He scratched the entire ticket to see where all the rest of the prizes were. The $200,000 was matched with a 5. One off from his winning number of 4. He scrunched his nose at the numbers and set the ticket down on the table. He downed more beer.

The lottery didn't seem to be working out and, truthfully probably wouldn't. He'd read the statistics about how many people went broke trying to hit the jackpot. He didn't care.

He sat back on the bed. He wasn't in the mood to smoke. He'd be out in another hour anyway. Maybe sooner depending on how fast he could down the beer.

Reggie thought thoughts about what he was going to do. He got up and opened the door. The night air was cool. No one was outside. He poked his head outside and looked in both directions. A couple of cars passed by the motel, but that was all.

He shut his door and sat back down.

How to get more money without selling drugs. Fair Zone was about to slow all the way down. He turned on the television to have some noise to help drown out his thoughts. He mindlessly flipped through the channels and stopped on a movie he'd seen a few times. It was a comedy. That was needed right now. He sat back and thought about work the next day. Maybe he'd get a few tips. But he hated relying on the generosity of others. And he shouldn't have to rely on tips to survive anyway. He thought about selling drugs again. He could go next door and get a few extra grams from Money and see what happened with that. No. Maybe he could get a part-time job at the motel. No. Everyone that worked in the motel were family. Or at least Indian minus the maids. But they didn't speak English and he was sure they were being exploited with cheap labor. He let the idea go as quickly as he thought of it.

Nothing of any value came to mind. He forgot about the movie altogether. He finished his beer and tossed the can in the trash can.

He turned off the light. The television screen lit the room. He saw lights flashing outside his door and went to the window. An ambulance had pulled in. There was no siren blaring, but the lights flashed intensely.

He wanted to wait to see who'd be hauled off in the back of the meat wagon, but the paramedics didn't seem to be in a rush. Tired of waiting, he laid back down. Nothing serious. The police nor the fire department had pulled up.

The beer kicked in a little more. He laid down and closed his eyes until he slept.

CHAPTER 19

Reggie balanced between eating his footlong turkey sub from Subway and keeping his eyes on the road. The start of another day at Fair Zone.

"You know that was some bullshit the other day right?" Dustin said.

He had purchased two bags of plain chips, a Tabasco Slim Jim, and two cans of Arizona Fruit Punch from the adjoining gas station.

"What?" Reggie asked between chewing.

"That cow that said we stole that hundred from her," Dustin said.

"Oh, right. Yeah. I forgot all about that. I will say that was my first time being accused of stealing from a customer," Reggie said and finished eating his sub. He sipped his fountain drink after.

Dustin was eating his Slim Jim.

"Has anybody ever really been caught?" Dustin said between bites.

"Caught what? Stealing? Sure. Henry told me about a guy who worked at the shop a few years ago. Can't remember his name but he wasn't very bright. At least it didn't sound like it from the story I heard," Reggie said.

"And? What happened?" Dustin prodded.

"From what Henry said it was a young guy. Hadn't been with the company long so he was still an assistant. While the crew chief was cleaning, the guy decided to wander around the house. The homeowner had left to run to the bank to get cash to pay for the cleaning. Can't remember if he left something, or just got back really fast, but he caught the assistant in his bedroom. The crew chief was cleaning the living room so there wasn't any reason for him to have been in that part of the house. The homeowner didn't say anything at the time, but he called the shop an hour or so after the crew left. Said he was missing a watch and other small shit. Chris popped up on the crew and found the items still in the assistants' pockets. The crew chief had no clue. He was fired on the spot" Reggie said.

"They call the cops?" Dustin asked.

"I didn't ask. I imagine if the homeowner wanted to press charges he could have though. With him being so young, I don't think Chris would've pushed it any further than firing if he wasn't pressed," Reggie said.

Dustin pondered the story in his mind. He cracked open one of his Arizona's and stared at the traffic on the interstate.

"Look-"

Reggie's voice broke through the silence that had settled in the van.

"-we work a job that requires us to be inside of people's homes. Shit happens. Don't rack ya brain. At the end of the day, people have a right to be insecure. We ain't there to make them feel safe. We're there to clean carpets," Reggie said.

With that, Reggie took another bite of his sub. Dustin remained quiet.

❄ ❄ ❄

It was Friday. Fair Zone didn't give the option for direct deposits, so every two weeks they handed out paper checks.

Reggie's check had been $100 less than normal the previous check. He'd had to buy fewer items from Dollar Tree to eat and make sure he was able to pay his weekly bill at Competitive Inn. He also needed enough for beer and weed. Unnecessary necessities to cope with life.

He'd been upset, but the drag of the slow season was just beginning.

Besides the loyal customers, a lot of the work went to Global Cleaners during the last major holidays of the year.

All twelve of the employees lined up in the Route Room and waited for Chris to hand out checks.

"I know my check ain't gonna be shit."

Larry walked up beside Reggie. Reggie knew he was high from how droopy and spaced out his eyes looked. He had sense enough to use eye drops to eliminate the redness, but one's eyes always told the condition of the mind.

"Why you say that?" Reggie asked.

He took precautions when discussing pay with the other employees. Management had told everyone the same thing after they were hired *Don't Discuss Pay With Anyone.* The only reason not to discuss pay was so they could maintain the nothing they were already paying you.

"I missed four days this check. My son was sick and his momma couldn't take off work. My sales ain't been shit either," Larry said.

"Mine was trash too," Reggie said. "Bout that time of year for us on top of that."

"I'm selling weed vape pens if you need one man. Or you can just buy the cartridges from me. I'm hustling this season bro," Larry said.

Reggie had no intention of buying from him. He hated vape pens. He liked his weed leafy, not liquid. He'd also seen that a few of the pens had blown up in people's faces. The most action he ever got from a blunt was the seeds popping if there were any. He had no intention of rearranging his face to get high.

"How much?" Reggie asked.

"$50 for the pen and cartridge. $30 for the cartridges by themselves. The pens are reusable though. Or you can buy a pen from a vape shop and just buy the cartridges from me. Just let me know and I got you either way," Larry said.

"Bet. I'm good right now, but I'll let you know," Reggie said.

Larry nodded.

"Gotta do something to make some extra bucks around here. You got another job?" Larry asked.

"No.," Reggie said

"How you survive?" Larry asked.

"I get by alright," Reggie said.

He was short. The conversation was getting more personal than he cared to discuss with Larry or any of the other employees. Larry sensed he may be prying and eased up.

"As long as you got something. This-"

"Reggie!"

Chris's voice cut Larry off. Reggie was relieved. He grabbed his check from Chris and then went to his van to see how much tighter he'd need to pull his belt.

❄ ❄ ❄

He'd only made base pay. And after state taxes and benefits, it was $50 less than his previous check.

Reggie stared at the check. He could scrape by on $725 for the next two weeks.

"Fucking bullshit," he said aloud.

This was the last check of November. One more month until the slow season officially took hold. He'd told Dustin to save his money but that didn't seem reasonable at this point. Dustin was making less than him as an assistant. If he was struggling, he only imagined what Dustin's checked looked like.

A year living in the motel weighed on him. Having a roof over your head helped to maintain his morale, but Reggie wanted what most people wanted: a comfortable living and someplace to call his own.

Dustin hopped in the van interrupting Reggie's thoughts.

"How yo' check lookin'? Mine was on some fuck shit," Dustin said as he pulled his check out of his pocket and unfolded it.

"Mine wasn't shit either," Reggie responded.

"How the fuck am I supposed to save this shit?" Dustin asked rhetorically. "This is a joke, right? And they expect me to bring this..this NOTHING home!" Dustin said staring bitterly at his check.

Reggie sensed Dustin's anger turning to tears. He didn't cry though. He buckled his seat belt and sat back in the seat.

Reggie put the gear shift next to the steering wheel in drive and pulled out of the shop.

❄ ❄ ❄

The day was uneventful. Reggie spent a majority of it upset about his money and wondering what he could do to increase his fortune.

Nothing solid came to mind.

He cleaned in a daze. He even let Dustin get some experience pushing the wand.

Cleaning was reserved for the crew chief. This was because if a customer called in to complain about a poorly cleaned room, the blame fell on them. The assistant was there to make the cleaning process as seamless as possible. Also to learn how to clean, how to engage with the customer, and how to sell.

Their last house had been empty. Reggie let Dustin clean the entire house. It took longer than necessary, but Reggie didn't care.

When the money wasn't right, the job be damned.

❄ ❄ ❄

He usually went back to his room after leaving work.

On this day, he'd decided to grab a beer and take the bus to the park. He kept his beer can concealed in the brown paper bag he'd gotten from the attendant.

It was twilight.

The last of the light from the sun danced atop the pond in the center of the park.

Reggie sat at a bench.

An Asian middle-aged gentleman was fishing a few benches away.

After he finished meticulously changing his bait, he cast his line out into the pond.

He reeled in, cast out once more, and let his pole rest beside him on the bench.

Reggie gazed at the orange bobber swaying back and forth from the ripples in the pond created by the spouts in the center.

He gulped his beer.

The sound of singing arose and took his attention away from the fisherman.

Across the pond, in the spot designated for family cookouts, birthday parties, and other gatherings, a group of Mexican friends and family had gathered.

In unison, they all sang.

Though Reggie couldn't make out the words, he could tell it was a jovial song from the way it was being sung. Maybe even a spiritual one. Faith in the Mexican community was important.

Reggie listened as his thoughts shifted to his money and current situation.

❊ ❊ ❊

Back in the room, Reggie pulled out his remaining two grams of weed, broke it down, and rolled all of it into his leaf cigar. He'd usually never roll up more than a .5 or so, but tonight was different.

He blew the first couple of puffs out in rings. All of it disseminated into a single cloud.

211

His mind wandered to thoughts of Breanna. He thought of how pretty her smile was and how good she had smelled to him when they had first met. He thought of the first time they had sex. How passionate it was.

A roach scuttled across the desk. He let it live on this night. Like him, he thought, it was just trying to survive.

The knock on his door made the roach hurry across the desk and Reggie jump slightly as he was pulled out of his thoughts.

He looked at the door not sure if he had really heard a knock or if he had only imagined it.

The knock came again. Light, but hard enough for him to register that the person on the other side meant for him to answer.

Reggie got up and opened the door.

A short, Mexican fiend stared at him.

"Money?" He asked nervously. His accent was thick and his English poor. Reggie could tell even saying *Money* had been a struggle.

Reggie, angry, almost cursed him out. He relented and pointed next door.

The Mexican man took off his hat and tipped his head apologizing for the disturbance. Reggie slammed the door without acknowledging the apology.

He sat back down on the bed and relit his blunt.

The drug game seems pretty prosperous The thought came to him suddenly. *He's employed all hours of the day.*

The news was on. He checked the time near the bottom crawl. 1:35 am.

Besides being annoyed that a fiend had knocked on his door this late at night, he was also intrigued by the idea that he could make money at any time during the day. He took another drag from his blunt.

"Fuck that," he said aloud as smoke billowed out of his nose. "I ain't in the mood to serve these crazy muh-fuckas all day."

And what if one of them went all nutty? He'd seen heroin addicts, dustheads, and crackheads growing up and knew if there was one person you couldn't trust it was a person strung out on drugs. A mad fiend was akin to a rabid dog.

He brushed off the thought and continued smoking his blunt.

CHAPTER 20

"Bruh, why is you tripping?"

Reggie was seated at the front of the public bus. Two men seated directly across from him were arguing. Reggie could tell there was tension by the look on their faces as they spoke, but they had mostly kept the bickering between them. The conversation had begun to take a turn for the worse and the men had begun raising their voices. Other passengers started to key in on the dispute as they caught wind of what was transpiring.

One of the men was wearing purple and lime green Nike Air Maxes with brown khakis, a white t-shirt, and a purple Lakers hat turned backward. The other man, bald-headed, was dressed in long camouflage pants a black t-shirt, and some low top black Air Force Ones. From what Reggie had been able to make out while involuntarily eavesdropping on their conversation, the guy wearing the brown khakis owed the guy wearing the camouflage pants $20.

"You been ducking me all week, nigga! I want my fucking money!" the man wearing the camouflage pants said.

"You know I got you bruh. Why is you acting like this?" the man wearing the brown khakis said.

"Give me my fucking money!"

Everyone's attention zeroed in on the altercation. Reggie saw the bus driver look in her rearview at the commotion, but she didn't say anything. She was waiting to see how far the argument would go before stepping in. He'd been on a bus that had pulled over and police were called because of a fight that happened between two passengers. It'd taken him an extra hour to get home. He hoped this situation wasn't headed in that direction.

The man wearing the brown khakis got up and switched seats.

"Man, fuck that $20. You tripping off that for what?" The man wearing the brown khakis said as he sat down in a seat a couple of rows back from where he was originally sitting.

"Bruh, what's up man?" The guy in the camouflage pants said.

The man wearing the brown khakis didn't want to fight. Reggie and everyone on the bus could tell that he was trying to avoid the situation while maintaining his ego.

The bus stopped at a light. The bus driver watched the exchange as she waited for the light to change.

"I got you big bruh. Stop tripping," the man wearing the brown khakis said.

"Fuck you!" yelled the man in the camouflage pants.

"Watch your mouth."

"Watch my mouth? I could just say fuck the money and fuck you up!" The man wearing the camouflage pants said and stood up.

The bus was quiet. The light turned green but the bus driver hesitated before pulling off. The man wearing camouflage pants, now standing, grasped the grab bar so as not to be thrown back into his seat. Heads swayed left to right as the bus finally started moving. Everyone was silent.

Finally, as he rocked back and forth on the grab bar, the man in the camouflage pants sat back down. The bus driver smiled. Reggie could tell she'd seen a lot of confrontations, but this was one of the rare occasions where things didn't end violently.

The man wearing camouflage pants turned his head every so often and looked at the man for the remainder of the ride.

❄ ❄ ❄

The bus pulled up to the light rail station two stops later and everyone got off.

216

He watched as the man wearing the khaki pants walked over to the bald guy to plead his case. From Reggie's perspective, he wasn't having any of what was being told to him, but he kept his composure. Reggie looked down once more as he took the steps up to the light rail and watched the men go their separate ways. Both had decided freedom and life over death today.

Reggie couldn't help but think the man's luck might run out in the near future. Owing money on the streets was a death sentence. Either pay your debts or have all debts settled for you permanently. Only God forgave the debtors. Dead men don't owe.

Reggie sat and waited for the light rail. There were a few individuals on the platform.

He thought about how it might be if he did decide to sell drugs. He wasn't sure whether the argument he witnessed was over drugs or not, but things could get spooky over $20. It wasn't worth it. He'd need to buy in bulk from Money anyways. He didn't need him thinking he was trying to take his customers. *I'd have to get him a job at Fair Zone then* he thought to himself and laughed. Too many variables and none seemed worth it. He threw the thought out of his mind for good.

❄ ❄ ❄

A few days passed and Reggie still hadn't figured a way to garner money. He'd even considered quitting Fair Zone altogether, but he'd learned from experience that quitting a job before getting another or at least having a potential

217

employer was the quickest way to end up homeless. He was already a hiccup away as it was in the current shit hole he lived in. But he only had warehouse experience. The pay for driving a forklift didn't increase. In some cases, the pay was less than he was currently making. And, when he thought about it, he didn't want to load and unload trucks. He'd seen some of the older workers and witnessed how it looked when their bodies started to shut down. He'd seen them rubbing their knees. Witnessed the look of anxiety on their faces because they knew, silently, this would be what eventually killed them. Back-breaking work day in and out for little to no pay. The only way to earn money was to take on more hours of back-breaking work. Nasty cycle. And he'd worked four warehouse jobs already.

When he worked in the warehouse of a popular mail carrier there had been an older gentleman by the name of Vince who worked three trucks down the line from Reggie's assigned unloading section.

Two months into the job, Vince hadn't shown up nor called in for a week. The usual policy was three days with a no-call no-show and you were automatically terminated. Vince had been with the company for fifteen years and not once had he ever pulled a no-call no-show so they had given him the benefit of the doubt and waited two more days hoping he'd show up eventually.

The manager called both his cellphone and his home number. Vince didn't answer either line so the

218

manager, who had established a relationship with Vince, went by his home for a wellness check and to see why he'd stop showing up for work. From what he told the crew, he saw Vince asleep on his sofa and kicked in the door when he didn't wake up when he knocked on the door or tapped on the window.

Vince was dead. The coroner determined he'd died Sunday night. Nobody had come to check on him. He sat dead for nearly a week.

Even though he never heard his death had anything to do with working in the warehouse, Reggie knew his body had broken down. He worked in that warehouse during the summer. The temperatures in the truck could reach over 100 degrees. He'd seen people quit mid-shift because they just couldn't take the heat.

"Fuck those mother fuckers," Reggie said aloud.

He stared up at the ceiling in his room and let his thoughts flow.

There was a dead roach smashed into the ceiling. Not by Reggie. The previous occupant did the honors of this grotesque mural. Reggie's eyes fixated on the dead roach.

A knock at the door stopped his train of thought. He popped up and answered the door.

Breanna smiled at him.

An unexpected visit, but not an unwelcome one. Reggie stepped to the side without saying a word. She sauntered past him into the room and he closed the door.

219

❄ ❄ ❄

The sex was needed. It had taken his mind off figuring out how to get out of Competitive Inn. At least momentarily. Reggie had rolled a joint and he and Breanna were passing it back and forth between them.

"I thought you may not have enjoyed me the last time," Breanna said.

Reggie choked on the smoke he was exhaling. "What'chu mean?" He said coughing.

"Haven't seen you since that night. I thought we had a good time," Breanna said.

"Nah. It ain't even like that baby," Reggie said.

Hearing him say baby softened her. Reggie noticed her changed expression.

"The slow season at work is coming up and I'm trying to figure out a way to make some extra cash. I've been trying to come up with something, but..," Reggie's voice trailed off.

"But what?"

"I don't know. I just need to figure something out, Reggie said.

"You tried asking for more hours?" Breanna asked.

"The business doesn't work like that. We work what's on the schedule for that day. Once we finish our route, we're done. So even though we are getting paid hourly, it really depends on how many jobs we have that day. Sales are getting rough. And with Christmas coming up, no one's trying to shell out any extra cash right now," Reggie said.

Breanna took a drag from the joint and passed it back to Reggie.

"If you need some money, I can help you out," she said.

"What?! Hell nah. I'm not taking no money from you," Reggie said.

Breana saw the genuine look of disgust on his face.

"Why not?" Breanna asked.

"No offense, but I don't feel comfortable accepting money from a woman," Reggie said bluntly.

"That's your dick talking ego man. I don't mind helping," Breanna said.

"Call it what you want, but I'm not accepting any money from you. I'm not even asking for any. I'm just venting to vent at the moment, to be honest. I'll be aight," Reggie said and took a deep drag from the joint. He patted it out in the ashtray next to the bed after.

"I just wanted to put it out there," Breanna said.

"And I appreciate that. But I'm fine. What you been up to?"

"Surviving. Just like everybody else," Breanna said without looking at him.

"And how do you do that?" Reggie prodded.

"Do what?"

221

She was dancing around the topic. Reggie knew that she was trying to get out of answering the question, but he didn't care. He'd learned that women were like pickle jars. Tough to open at first, but if you give em' a couple pats on the ass, they'd eventually pop.

"You know what I'm asking. What do you do for a living?" Reggie said.

Breanna didn't say anything. She turned to him and put her hand on his chest and ran her fingers up until she got to his chin, lifted it, and looked him in the eyes.

"Listen, I'll tell you at some point, but I'll be the one to tell you. You won't have to keep asking me," Breanna said.

He wasn't satisfied with her response. He wanted to dig deeper into this mystery woman he was lying next to. And at the same time, if it was that big of a secret, maybe he didn't want to know. This was Competitive after all. He saw the genuine "drop it" look on her face and decided to let it go.

"You're making me feel like I'm sleeping with an undercover or something," Reggie said.

Breanna grabbed the joint from the ashtray and relit it. She took a drag and blew the smoke in his face.

"Does that ease your mind?" She said smiling at him.

"Nope," he responded playfully.

She took another drag and passed the joint back to him.

"I know something that might," she said coyly.

With that, she went under the sheet. Reggie took one more drag and patted the joint out in the ashtray. He exhaled laid back and closed his eyes.

CHAPTER 21

December brought with it the cold to the southeastern part of the country. And all the pressures of the Christmas season ushered in a new ferocity to the importance of making a dollar.

Reggie was used to the sight.

Stores filled with stressed individuals hoping they'd made enough for the year to splurge on gifts their recipients may only pretend to like.

Dustin sat in the passenger seat staring out the window at the houses as they drove to their first job. They'd been given a wealthy family on their route. The trees in the neighborhood were large. A telltale sign that this was one of the older neighborhoods in the city. Charlotte had a lot of new neighborhoods that were accentuated by the size of the trees and shrubbery in the yards and the neighborhood in general.

Reggie backed into the driveway of the two-story home. They were holiday folks. He could tell by all the lights, decorations, and the nativity scene in the middle of the front yard.

The large brick house was set down a winding drive. Reggie noted a guest house around back as he backed into the driveway.

James Wright was the name of the man who owned the home. Reggie noted this as he studied the cleaning history.

James was in the front yard readjusting baby Jesus in the manger when the Fair Zone van pulled up. He waved to the two men and kept adjusting.

"I think we may be here for a minute. Looks like they're getting all of their carpets cleaned and the tile in the kitchen too," Reggie said.

"Hopefully they tip good," Dustin said.

"They're spending over $600 already. They got a little money, but rich people don't usually tip good so I wouldn't bank on that," Reggie said.

"Well shit," Dustin said.

"That's just what I've seen. But it is Christmas time so we'll see," Reggie said.

"I got you. Just thinking out loud," Dustin said. He took a swig from his Fruit Punch flavored Gatorade.

Reggie finished looking at the Client History.

"You ready?" Reggie asked.

"Yup," Dustin said.

Dustin grabbed the chip bucket and they both climbed out of the van.

"What's up fellas," James said looking at the two men.

He was a middle-aged White man. Balding at the crown, the sternness of his facial features gave the hint that he had a firm hold on life. His face was friendly and carefree.

"How you doing today?" Reggie said.

"Oh, I'm alright. Just getting in the holiday spirit," James said. "You fellas care for a cup of coffee?"

"I'm good," Reggie responded.

"No thanks," Dustin said.

"I'm definitely not envious of your electric bill," Reggie said making a joke.

"Christmas comes once a year. I don't mind the extra expenses. The family loves all this stuff so I put it up every year. Keeps the boss happy anyways," James said pointing at the door.

Reggie knew the *boss* that James was referring to was his wife.

"I got you. Happy wife happy life, right?" Reggie said and smiled.

"Exactly," James responded with a smile.

"What are we doing here for you today?" Reggie asked.

"Getting all the floors in the house cleaned. You'll need to pull your van around back to clean the carpet in the guest house. Not much in there, but I might as well get everything done while I got you guys out here," James said.

"That's no problem. You wanna show us what we're cleaning inside before we get started?" Reggie asked.

"Sure, come on in," James said and led the way to the house.

Reggie and Dustin followed behind.

❄ ❄ ❄

Dustin didn't normally speak during walkthroughs unless necessary, but he was particularly silent this time. He was taken aback by the magnitude of the home. The entrance had black and white marble floors. An old piano sat in the corner beside the staircase that led to the upstairs. Vintage paintings gave a Victorian feel, though the house was modern for the most part.

James was a big game hunter and a taxidermy enthusiast. In his study was a full-size baboon he killed on a hunting trip in Africa that stood on its hind legs with its teeth on full display. Reggie stood in front of it and was surprised to be standing face to face. He didn't realize the size they could reach having never seen one in real life.

Body stuffed and eyes marbled, Reggie could still feel the intensity of the wild staring into the eyes of this dead primate.

James was showing Dustin a picture of a black bear he had killed on a hunting trip in Alaska. Reggie

227

noted the other animals in the room, but the baboon had taken residence in his mind. It was the wild intensity of the eyes. Even after death. Cause the eyes always tell the condition of the mind.

Being on the African plain having to fight for survival amongst other baboons. Food, shelter, a mate. The constant looming threat from other animals. And then you're killed by someone that doesn't even operate within your paradigm. The chaos of life was forever locked into the eyes of this baboon.

Reggie felt a sadness for the animal. He was staring at himself. Locked in a vicious cycle only to be killed by outsiders that had no skin in the game being played.

"Ready to check out the other rooms?" James asked.

His voice almost made Reggie jump.

"Yeah," Reggie said.

He took one last look at the animal and left.

❅ ❅ ❅

They got started after the walkthrough. It took 20 minutes with the size of the house and getting James to sign the "Slip & Fall" notice. James didn't show them the guest house. He left it unlocked so they could pull the van around and clean it once they were done with the house. It wasn't as big and Reggie was ready to start cleaning anyway so he was relieved to skip that part of the tour.

Exhausted and dripping sweat from the heat of the steam hose, Reggie climbed into the van. He'd put the vacuum hose back on the van and unhooked the steam line. He pulled the van around back to clean the guest house.

Dustin walked the chip bucket and steam line to the guest house.

Like the main house, it was brick with burgundy shutters. A garden devoid of any fruit or vegetation was planted in front. A summer garden Reggie surmised. But, like the main house, the outside was maintained and clean.

"Almost done," Reggie said to Dustin as he stepped out of the van.

"I like speed cleaning, but I don't mind today. This is a nice fucking house man," Dustin said.

"Yeah, it is," Reggie said.

"How much you think it cost?" he asked.

"In this neighborhood? Million dollar house easily," Reggie said.

"That's what I was thinking," Dustin said. "I need me a place like this. Shooting big fucking animals for fun and shit and putting them in my study. Rich people shit."

Reggie's mind wandered back to the baboon and the look of chaos in its eyes. *Rich people shit* he thought to himself.

"We ain't buying no house that looks like this with Fair Zone paychecks," Reggie said.

"I know. But one day man. Seeing shit like this ain't motivational for you?" Dustin said.

"This house? No. But the freedom to do what you want is," Reggie said.

"I just want the money," Dustin said.

"And that's good enough. Hook up that steam line. I'm gonna drag the vac hose in so we can get outta here. It's gonna be lunchtime soon and cleaning this house got me hungry," Reggie said.

"Cool. I can eat right now too," Dustin said.

❄ ❄ ❄

He cleaned the tile in the small kitchenette first. Next was the tile in the bathroom. James mentioned that the guest house was rarely used. How quickly the floors cleaned up confirmed this.

Reggie started cleaning the bedroom after. He thrust the wand under the bed to clean in his normal fashion but heard a clicking noise after the third thrust.

Items sometimes got caught in the wand so he didn't think much of it.

He flipped the wand to see what was causing the jam once he'd unhooked the vacuum hose.

A diamond bracelet was stuck in the wand.

"Oh shit," he said louder than he wanted to.

Dustin came over to inspect. Seeing the bracelet he paused.

"Oh shit," Dustin said.

Reggie took caution in easing the bracelet out of the wand.

All of the diamonds were still intact. They both stared in amazement.

"That bracelet is at least 10 bands," Dustin said.

"Yeah," Reggie responded without taking his eyes off of the bracelet.

Dustin said what they both were thinking after a while.

"You gonna give it back?" He asked.

Reggie's first instinct was to say yes, but he was quiet. He'd never held this amount of money. In the form of currency or otherwise.

"James said they don't really use the guest house. No telling how long this bracelet's been in here and nobody noticed it was here. Or even missing. Pawning this could add a few extra gifts under the tree for you and your girlfriend. And it'd pay for a nice crib for the little one," Reggie said.

He understood he wasn't trying to convince himself, but Dustin.

"It definitely could," Dustin said.

"We'll probably get about four thousand for it. Pawnshops are shit. But that's two thousand more than either one of us has," Reggie said.

"Free money is free money. Would damn sure make up for those short checks we been getting," Dustin said.

"You better not fucking mention this to anyone. We're both on the hook here. Keep your fucking mouth shut," Reggie said.

Dustin knew he was serious. If they did get caught, it'd mean more than their jobs. Especially if the bracelet was worth as much as they thought it was.

"I ain't saying shit," Dustin said.

Reggie eyed Dustin and nodded once he was satisfied. They looked at the bracelet again. Reggie put it in his pocket and they finished cleaning.

❄ ❄ ❄

He took the bus to Kannapolis to find a pawnshop. It was 30 minutes from the city and Reggie figured it'd be best not to try any of the shops he usually went to.

He'd received no suspicious looks. The current climate of the country was one in turmoil. There were plenty of individuals pawning their valuables for what little they could get in return. Reggie had seen talks of a recession on the news. That didn't mean much to him. Every day was a recession.

He hadn't been told how much the bracelet was worth, but they gave him $4500. He pocketed the extra $500. He was the crew chief after all which raised the stakes for him if they were caught.

❄ ❄ ❄

It was dark when he got back to the city. He took the light rail to the AMC Theatre parking lot to meet Dustin.

Reggie saw his red Dodge Ranger truck parked underneath a tree. He approached and tapped on the window. Dustin unlocked the door.

"You did it?" Dustin said as Reggie sat down.

"We wouldn't be here if I didn't," Reggie said.

He pulled out $2000 and handed it to Dustin. His eyes lit up once he held the money.

Reggie could see the excitement on his face. But there was also something else. Something feral.

"What you thinking about?" Reggie asked.

"This money," Dustin said.

"Is that all?" Reggie asked.

"What else is there to think about?" Dustin said.

"This ain't gotta be the last time. Especially with what's about to happen next month. I'm not saying we're gonna be casing houses, but we can come up for a couple months off these rich folks. At least until work picks up again," Reggie said.

It was an idea he'd developed on the bus ride back from Kannapolis. In his mind, he'd be able to make enough to get out of Competitive.

"You serious?" Dustin asked.

"Look, we could both use the money. And, if we're smart, this money could do more than just get us through the slow season," Reggie said.

Dustin stared at the money in his hand. Reggie could see he was coming to grips with the possibilities.

Before Dustin responded, Reggie spoke again.

"Enjoy your Christmas. We'll talk more after the holidays. After you see what that little bit you got in your hand does for you," he said.

Reggie got out of the truck and Dustin pulled off. He honked his horn as he drove away.

Reggie walked back to the light rail.

❄ ❄ ❄

Members from one of the local churches knocked on everyone's door at the motel around 9 am to offer breakfast on Christmas morning.

Reggie declined. He didn't trust what everyone did in their kitchen. And frankly, people weren't trustworthy in general. How easy would it be to kill off an entire slew of individuals that no one gave a damn about than under the guise of fellowship?

The movies stayed open on Christmas and so did Chinese restaurants. Reggie had already asked Breanna if she had any plans.

They agreed to spend the day together.

He knocked on her door a little before noon. She answered with a smile wearing form-fitting blue jeans with a long-sleeve white plunge blouse that exposed her cleavage and a brown cardigan sweater for the cold. Her make-up was done and she'd gotten micro braids.

She looked like someone else to Reggie. He was taken by her for a moment.

"You look amazing Bri," he said.

"Thank you," Breanna said blushing.

Reggie took her in for a moment longer, grabbed her by the hand, and they left.

❄ ❄ ❄

They decided on a horror movie. Reggie was surprised by how much she enjoyed it.

"Shit like that doesn't bother you, huh?" Reggie asked as they walked back to the light rail.

"I watched Candyman when I was little at my cousins' house. Her mom had it on VHS so we snuck and watched it. I didn't sleep at all that night, but I've been hooked since. The new stuff ain't that great, to be honest. It's more gross-out than horror," Breanna said.

It was the first time Reggie had heard Breanna mention anything about her personal life. She might be falling for him after all he thought.

"That's the one with Tony Todd?" He asked.

"Yeah. He's probably my favorite Black actor in the genre," she said.

They paused at the intersection. Reggie pushed the button for the crosswalk light to allow them to cross. Traffic was almost nonexistent, but they weren't in a rush to go anywhere.

"Thanks for inviting me out," Breanna said as they waited.

"Of course. Glad you accepted the invitation," he said.

"I can't remember the last time I spent the holiday with someone," Breanna said smiling at him.

Her last remark was only a partial truth. Breanna hadn't spent the last couple of Christmas's with a romantic interest, she'd spent them with one of her clients. She always made extra on holidays as her Damon's were in the giving mood.

They just wanted company for the most part. Lonely men who either couldn't make it home to their families or just men who wanted to feel like someone cared. Even for a day. And even if they had to pay for the company.

❄ ❄ ❄

Reggie ate at the Dragon Express Chinese restaurant a few times before. The food was good and, more importantly, they were open.

An older Black couple was seated in the far corner eating. They talked and smiled at one another while they ate.

Reggie ordered his go-to. White rice and wings. Breanna ordered lo mein, mixed vegetables, and peppered steak.

"How's work going?" Breanna asked.

"Work is work," Reggie said. "Not much to talk about really."

"How's the job hunt going?"

"Job hunt?"

"You said you wanted another job," Breanna said.

"No, I said I needed more money. That part's going fine. Making more money. I'm not trying to bounce around. They not paying shit anywhere. One job is just as good as the next in this city," Reggie said and took a bite of one of his chicken wings.

"That's true. But it sounds like you secured the bag," Breanna said.

There was nothing secure about what Reggie and Dustin were about to get into. They would be thrown in prison or murdered if they got caught by a gun-owning homeowner. But with great risks come great rewards. The phrase resonated in his mind even though it was a dark take on the popular line.

"Something like that," he replied.

"I get it. Don't wanna jinx it. I'm happy for you though babe," Breanna said.

"Maybe I can take you somewhere out of the city," Reggie said.

"Like where?" She asked.

"Anywhere. Just to get away. Even if it's only for a few days," he said.

"I'd go anywhere with you," Breanna said and smiled. There was broccoli in her teeth.

Reggie motioned her to clean it out. She pulled a tiny mirror out of her purse, found where the broccoli was stuck and picked it out with her pinky nail.

He laughed a little as she did this.

They ate and talked for about two hours before leaving. The older couple left an hour before they did. Besides them, no one else came into the restaurant.

CHAPTER 22

The holidays passed and winter took hold. Reggie and Dustin sat in the parking lot of a McDonald's discussing the best way to carry out their scheme. They weren't professionals. But he at least wanted to make sure they weren't going in completely blind.

"So how do we get the stuff out of the house?" Dustin asked.

Reggie never hung out with any of the employees outside of work, but things like this couldn't be discussed at work in great enough length and he needed to be sure everything was understood. Though he needed the money, he had no plans of going to prison.

Reggie sat still thinking.

Dustin twiddled his thumbs but didn't speak.

"The chip bucket," Reggie said.

"What?" Dustin asked.

"I don't know. Think about it. We're not stealing t.v.'s, furniture, or big bulky shit like that. We can put jewelry and smaller stuff in the chip bucket. You can walk it back to the van without raising any suspicion from the customers too. If we come across any money, maybe we take that too. But people tend to notice missing money quickly. Especially when someone has been in their home. We've both seen that firsthand, remember?" Reggie asked.

Dustin nodded, remembering the encounters they'd had over the past few weeks.

"All these houses we clean, we'll make a killing off of jewelry alone and any other small shit we can fit in the chip bucket," Reggie said.

Dustin continued twiddling while he thought about Reggie's idea. Reggie waited patiently. He could tell Dustin had all but made up his mind. He just needed his mouth to follow suit with his thoughts.

A smile came across his face.

"Okay. What's the split?" Dustin asked.

"Fifty-fifty. There's no need in one pot being bigger than the other since we're taking the same risk," Reggie said.

It was around midnight. A car pulled up to the drive-thru while they conversed. Activity around the restaurant was light otherwise.

Reggie noticed one of the workers standing on the side of the building smoking a cigarette.

The grin on Dustin's face told him all he needed to know, but he still wanted verbal confirmation that he understood how the plan was to be carried out.

Dustin was momentarily lost in thought. When a man had the ability to make more money than he imagined, and quick, his thinking switched and he'd easily get lost in thought about what he would do with his newfound fortune.

Reggie began to grow impatient.

"So..?" Reggie pressed.

Dustin turned and looked him in the eyes.

"I'm all in."

❄ ❄ ❄

Headed to the first house on their route, Reggie and Dustin were silent. There was no turning back. They'd gone over the plans and both knew what each other's job was. Reggie maintained focus on the road. He didn't have an appetite, so he hadn't stopped for his normal sub. He'd asked Dustin whether he wanted to stop, but he said he didn't have much of an appetite either.

Dustin had looked nervous to Reggie, but he expected that. He too was nervous. If anything went wrong today, they'd be finished before they even got started. Dustin did have more to lose with his pregnant girlfriend at home but Reggie hoped that would keep him focused on the goal.

He spent the drive shaking off the nervous energy and hoped Dustin was doing the same. They would be using this money to get them both out of the precarious situations they found themselves in, in their individual lives.

He glanced over at Dustin out of the corner of his eye. He had turned and was staring out of the window.

Reggie had cleaned the chip bucket at the shop and made sure they weren't carrying any unnecessary items. He grabbed extra rags as well. They could use the rags to cover any of the items they took in the chip bucket. He'd thought of that while he was setting up the van.

Reggie figured Dustin knew that there was no turning back from what they were about to do, but right in the thick of things, he wanted to give Dustin one last out. He was also giving himself an out because if Dustin decided against it, he'd scrap the plan altogether and they'd never speak of it again.

"I know you know this, but I'm gonna say this one time and I won't be asking again," Reggie started. "If you have any hesitations about what we're getting into, say so now. We can forget the plan and work the jobs like normal. Chalk this up to desperate talk between desperate men and nothing more."

Dustin had taken his attention from looking out the window and looked over at Reggie. He didn't say anything after Reggie finished speaking. He focused his attention on the road.

Reggie hadn't taken his eyes off the road and had spoken to Dustin without looking at him. He waited for Dustin's response in silence.

"I'm not some church boy or anything, but I know stealing shit from people is wrong. The thing is, with this little bit of money I'm making, I feel like I'm being robbed every day. I thought about it all night. Hell, I've been thinking bout it all morning too. You have too I'm sure. And I keep coming to the same conclusion. I need the money. I hope I'm pardoned when I die if you believe in that sort of thing. But the short answer is I'm not changing my mind now," Dustin said.

Reggie gripped the steering wheel tighter. In some weird way, he was inspired by Dustin's speech. He didn't respond. He didn't need to.

❆ ❆ ❆

The first house was an older couple. The Hoffman's. They lived in a large two-story stone house. Reggie could tell they were both northerners from their accent.

"The two of you can lift that table off the area rug and clean it as well," Mrs. Hoffman said.

Her husband was seated staring at SportsCenter highlights. He wasn't paying attention to what his wife was saying nor did he look like he could be bothered.

Reggie could tell they'd been married for years. The wife took the reigns in this relationship. At least when it came to the decisions in the house.

"I also spilled some make-up next to the dresser in our bedroom. I tried my best to get it out, but I think it may have stained the carpet. See what you can do to get that up for me please," she said.

"We have a few products that might work. I'll see what I can do and let you know once we're finished," Reggie said.

"Alright. Thank you," she said.

Mr. Hoffman got up from his chair. He rose slowly and labored.

"We gotta head out for a bit. Got a few errands to run. We should be back before you fellas get finished," Mr. Hoffman spoke now for the first time since Reggie and Dustin had entered their home.

"I'll leave my number on the counter. Just give me a buzz if we're not back yet. We're just going up the road to the grocery store and the bank. Shouldn't take too long," he said.

They lucked out. Reggie knew instinctually without looking at Dustin that they were thinking the same thing. With them leaving they'd have enough time to do the job and claim a prize. There was less pressure with them out of the house. Even if it was only for a little while.

"That's fine. We'll probably still be cleaning by the time you two get back. Looks like we're going to need a lot of hose for those back bedrooms on the second floor," Reggie said.

"Park your van closer to the door. That's what the other technicians do when they come out to clean. Your hose should stretch pretty far if I remember correctly. Watch out for the furniture when you get to the landing, but there's not much stuff in the hallway," Mr. Hoffman said.

Mrs. Hoffman had left the living room and was grabbing her purse off the kitchen counter.

"You need anything else from us?" she said walking back into the living room.

"No, I think we're good to get started," Reggie said.

"Alright, we'll go on and get out of your way," Mr. Hoffman said.

The four of them walked to the door. The Hoffman's to run their errands and Reggie and Dustin to set up the van for the job.

❊ ❊ ❊

They started cleaning in the master bedroom. After they had drug the vacuum hose and steam line into the room, they began looking around.

There were a lot of things in the bedroom, but most of it was big stuff and stuff that wouldn't fetch anything at a pawn shop.

Jewelry was what they were after. Mrs. Hoffman didn't keep any of her jewelry in plain sight. He noticed this as soon as they stepped into the room. Most people didn't so this wasn't surprising.

He saw the make-up that Mrs. Hoffman was referring to. It looked like it had stained the carpet, but he poured some citrus onto the spot to help loosen the make-up from the fibers. At the very least he would be able to get the spot to lighten, though it'd take a rinse and repeat process to do it. He reminded himself to advise her to put a small area rug over it if she couldn't stand to look at the stain.

Dustin looked in the walk-in closet, but it was only filled with dresses, suits, shoes, and hats. Nothing that they wanted to put on the van.

"See anything in there," Reggie called out as Dustin checked the closet.

"No, nothing. Just some clothes," he said as he ran his hand along Mrs. Hoffman's dresses. "They got some expensive-looking clothes though. Too bad my girl can't fit none of this stuff."

"They don't buy clothes at the pawnshop. Leave a note for them to donate to Good Will if you want, but keep looking in the meantime," Reggie said poking his head in the closet.

"Fuck you," Dustin said chuckling a little at Reggie's humor.

"I'm going to get started cleaning so we're not wasting too much time," Reggie said.

The Hoffman's were old, so Reggie knew it was just a matter of finding where they kept their expensive jewelry. Dustin had the same feeling. He turned off the light in the closet and stepped out.

Reggie walked over to the wand and began cleaning.

There were pictures of the Hoffman's at various points of their life, kids, and grandkids around the room.

Reggie studied a picture of the couple in front of the Brooklyn bridge.

They were young and the day was sunny. She had one of those Marilyn Monroe-looking scarfs tied around her head. Mr. Hoffman was dressed like a young professional. There were two ladies taking pictures of the bridge standing off to the side. Reggie recognized the Fujifilm camera both ladies were using to take the picture.

"Found something," Dustin said.

Reggie turned around and saw Dustin had pulled out one of the drawers on the dresser where the make-up stain was.

Reggie approached as Dustin ruffled through the drawer.

"What'd you find?" Reggie asked.

Dustin pulled out a pair of teardrop red ruby earrings.

"And voila," Dustin said showing Reggie the earrings.

They looked expensive alright.

"Where's the chip bucket?" Reggie asked.

"Downstairs," Dustin said.

"Bring it up and we'll fold this into one of the rags so they don't get damaged," Reggie said.

Dustin turned on his heel and bolted out of the room.

Reggie heard him racing down the steps to retrieve the chip bucket.

He stared at the earrings. They were nice. This was a good sign in his mind. There was now less pressure to case the rest of the house. No need to steal a ton of stuff. One very expensive item would do. He'd make sure to relay this message to Dustin when he came back upstairs.

Dustin entered the room chip bucket in hand. He took one of the rags out of the bucket and handed it to Reggie.

Reggie placed the earrings into the rag and folded it. He set the rag in the corner of the bucket and moved the other products closer to keep them in place.

"Alright, cool," Reggie said. "Let's just finish up cleaning. If we come across something else, maybe, but this is probably good enough for one house."

Dustin's breathing had increased. Reggie could tell the action excited him. Understandable. His pulse was racing. He made sure he stuffed the earrings tight enough into the bucket and handed it to Dustin.

"Keep it in the room," Reggie said slowly handing the chip bucket to Dustin as though it contained a life saving antibiotic.

Dustin walked the bucket over to the door and set it down. He closed the dresser drawer and went back to stand next to the bucket.

Reggie picked up the wand and finished cleaning.

❄ ❄ ❄

They kept the ruby earrings as their only prize for the day. The next house had been an Indian couple. The husband had followed them around the entire time they were in their home.

Reggie had expected this. They weren't pressed to take from every house.

They finished cleaning and left quickly.

They still considered the day a success.

CHAPTER 23

There Is No Us Without You.

Reggie stood outside of Fair Zone reading the sign. Though he'd seen it hundreds of times before, the sign now seemed to take on an ominous tone. Like the managers had come up with the phrase to spite the workers.

We Don't Get Rich Without You it should've read if that were the case he thought and laughed.

It also reminded him of a quote he'd seen posted on the church where he'd grown up. It was identical to the point Reggie was sure they'd taken a variation of the phrase to come up with the quote he was now staring at.

There Is No Sin Without You.

He thought the phrase was too dark to be posted on a church billboard, but it was right.

There is no sin without YOU.

He stared at the sign as it twirled around on the pole like the strippers at *The Muse* that he'd visited a few times since he'd been staying at Competitive.

There Is No Sin Without You.

He only saw this phrase now.

Two Mexican kids rode by on their bikes. Reggie caught wind of their conversation.

"Nigga, shut up."

"I'm telling you. That bitch was into me."

"You don't get no pussy."

"Yes, I do nigga."

The kids continued by.

Reggie was pretty used to hearing the younger Mexicans use the word nigga. They were brown people just like him. And whatever. Minority wars never made much sense to him. Both only gained a better position at the bottom.

Reggie watched the sign spin a few more times and went to clock in.

❄ ❄ ❄

The feeling of death was heavy in the tiny apartment.

Claire hadn't mentioned that her husband had overdosed on alcohol the night before on the gray chenille sofa Reggie and Dustin were now staring at when they did the walkthrough.

In her late thirties, Claire was a green-eyed blonde-haired White female that reminded Reggie of

251

every southern White girl he'd known growing up(minus the green eyes).

Reggie saw how solemn she was while staring at the vomit on and in front of the sofa.

She wasn't grossed out. There was pity in her stare.

They pulled the sofa away from the wall and Reggie cleaned it first.

Dustin was in the kitchen with Claire while Reggie was cleaning. Reggie noticed the look on Dustin's face as they spoke.

She went to the bathroom and Dustin came over to Reggie and told him what they were talking about.

"Fuck," Reggie said after hearing the story.

"He'd been an alchi for a while. Tried to quit, you know, but couldn't get the monkey off his back," Dustin said.

"And he choked on his own vomit?" Reggie asked.

"Yeah. She'd gone to bed for the night. Got up to pee and saw he wasn't next to her. Came out and saw the vomit and just figured he was too drunk to make it to the bathroom. Got the shock of her life when he wouldn't wake up," Dustin said keeping his voice low.

"Fuck," Reggie said again.

"He was tipsy when she went to bed. Still in his right mind though. She's all torn up. He was a drunk, but he wasn't punchy. Just had his demons," Dustin said and shook his head.

Reggie shook his head as well and connected the upholstery cleaning tool to the vacuum hose.

Claire walked out of the bedroom. Eyes red and holding kleenex, she sat down at the table in the kitchen and stared at the wall.

Reggie and Dustin glanced at each other and then over at Claire. He made a point to make sure both the sofa and carpet were spotless.

After he finished cleaning, Reggie deodorized for free. She hadn't purchased deodorizer, but Reggie wanted to make sure the smell didn't seep back up. Bad enough she'd have to look at the spot where her husband died. She'd probably move before long he figured.

She was able to pull herself together to thank them for the job. She tried to tip, but they both refused.

Dustin was holding a picture frame filled with two-dollar bills.

"What about this?"

Reggie guessed there to be about $100 altogether give or take. Money was money, but he knew the homeowners would notice so he decided against it.

No need to steal things that would get them caught off the bat.

"Put it back. They'll notice it too soon and we're finished," Reggie said motioning for Dustin to slide the frame back underneath the bed.

"Put it back?" Dustin asked.

"Put it back goddammit. I don't plan on getting caught for stupid shit. There's gotta be easier shit to steal. If not, we'll move on to the next house," Reggie said.

Dustin understood but his youth wanted to take everything in sight. Reluctantly, he slid the frame back under the bed.

A week into their side vocation and things were going smoothly. There hadn't been any calls into the shop about anyone missing items. Reggie credited himself for this. He'd made sure that whatever they took was the least likely to be noticed. That or, by the time they'd realized a pair of earrings, a watch, necklace, bracelet, or whatever they swiped was missing, the homeowner would figure they'd misplaced it rather than suspecting two carpet cleaners had robbed their home.

Reggie had second guessed his decision during this first week. Stealing from people who had earned their possessions and their lifestyle was wrong and he knew it. He'd never fancied himself a thief. When he was elementary school age, he and his friends would steal candy from the local corner store, but that was the extent of his life of crime up until this point. But in this new America, where sink or swim was the motto for its working-class citizens and the government had forgotten about the clock workers who made her tick, he was determined to survive and, if necessary, take his slice of the American pie.

He wasn't a killer and had no plans of becoming one. This wasn't a stick-up operation like the bandits from the old American west. Nor was it a smash and grab as jewelry store heist had devolved into. In his mind, this was a take what you need kind of affair that would yield no casualties.

And once the first week of April rolled around they'd stop. By then he planned to have a sizable amount of money stashed away to be able to leave Fair Zone, get his own place to live and move his life in a different direction.

He never shared any of this with Dustin. He'd noticed a shift in his attitude since they'd started. Reggie chalked it up to youth but that youthful ignorance and blind courage had the potential to unravel the entire operation if allowed to spring up at an inopportune moment.

He knew he'd need to keep an eye on Dustin and pull back the reigns when need be.

But for now, everything was just fine.

❅ ❅ ❅

A month passed and Reggie hadn't seen Breanna as much, but with the money he was making, he didn't mind. She wasn't his and with her reluctance to say what she did for a living, Reggie figured there were skeletons in her closet that still had some life in them.

Dustin had the day off so he was solo. The master bedroom and a hallway were all that was scheduled on his last house on his route. He hadn't seen anything worth taking in the previous three homes, but he wasn't pressed either.

Reggie noticed earrings sitting on the sink in the bathroom when he stopped to pee while he was cleaning the bedroom. He didn't take them partially because they were out in the open, but mainly because he didn't want to.

His instincts almost made him grab them anyway. Over the course of the month, Reggie could see why killers killed. Instinct. Whether you wanted to or not, once something got into your bones, there was no denying the urge.

As sick as it was, he thought to himself, that was the reality. He stared at the earrings as he finished peeing and washing his hands.

❄ ❄ ❄

Reggie had gone by Smiley's after work for his nightly beers. He switched the brand up from time to time, but for the most part, Budweiser's did the trick. Unless he was flat broke. In which case an Edge or Steel Reserve 211 would suffice. He hated the slight hangovers from Malt liquor, but it was manageable.

"How you doing Chinedu?"

Chinedu was in her usual place; seated behind the glass at the register.

"How you doing my friend?" She responded.

"I'm good," he said.

Chinedu didn't usually work nights so Reggie figured her husband either had something else to do or he had gotten sick.

"Where's the muscle?" He asked.

Chinedu burst out laughing.

"Ah, you're so funny. The muscle is at home resting. He's been ill the last few days. I told him to go see a doctor, but he is stubborn," she said.

"Oh. Well, I hope he gets better soon. I know you don't like working here late," Reggie said.

"No. But I don't mind. It's usually the same customers so I'm not afraid," she said. "I'd rather be at home in my bed watching Golden Girls. I love those ladies. So funny."

"Believe it or not, I use to watch that show coming up. Been a minute since I've seen it though," Reggie said.

Reggie paused and they both said simultaneously, "Picture it". They shared a laugh. She rang up his beer and hot pork rinds.

"You enjoy your night," Reggie said as he grabbed his bag.

"You do the same," she said and watched him walk out of the store.

❄ ❄ ❄

Early the next morning, there was a knock at the door.

Reggie was watching the highlights from the basketball games the night before. A combination of beer and exhaustion had put him to sleep before halftime of the first game.

He waited to see whether the kids at the motel were playing a game of knock and run. The knock came again.

Reggie got up and answered the door.

Isaac stood on the other side.

"How are you doing?" He asked.

"All good. What's up?"

Isaac didn't come to individual rooms other than to collect rent or to check on the odd complaint that may come his way pertaining to the room (toilet backed up, air conditioner not working, etc.).

Reggie kept smoking during the day in the room to a minimum for this very reason. It'd be both maddening and expensive if he got put out for smoking weed.

"Everything in the room working good?" Isaac asked.

The question caught Reggie off guard. He hadn't put in a complaint and everything, at least to his knowledge, was working just fine.

"As far as I know. Nothing's given me any trouble recently," he said.

"Good," Isaac said.

"Y'all been getting a lot of complaints or something?" Reggie asked.

"Not really. Just going around and making sure all the rooms are up to par. Try and stay ahead, ya know? So many people come in and out. It's hard to keep up with maintenance at times," Isaac said.

"Got you. No complaints from - oh," Reggie said interrupting himself. "I need to come down to the office to grab a couple extra rolls of toilet paper," Reggie said.

"I'll be back in the office after I'm through making my rounds," Isaac said.

"Okay," Reggie said.

Just then a man carrying an infant child walked around the corner and up the stairs. He was flanked by two toddler-age children and his girlfriend brought up the rear.

Isaac and Reggie observed the family make their way to their room.

"I don't understand that," Isaac said.

"What do you mean?" Reggie asked.

"How you can have children when you live in this condition. He's not working full time and can barely make his weekly rent. I think it's selfish and irresponsible. Children deserve smarter parents," he said.

Reggie took in the words. He wasn't offended and even agreed with the assessment. It was just weird to hear it coming from an Indian man.

"You're not wrong," he said after a moment.

Reggie never paid the families he saw much attention. He'd seen plenty come and go. None no worse off than the next. Competitive Inn made everyone equal.

Isaac's words made him think.

"Seems like a sad way to live," Isaac said.

Reggie nodded in acknowledgment of this last remark. The boyfriend stepped out of the room and lit a cigarette.

"I have to finish my rounds. Come to the office in 20 minutes for tissue," Isaac said.

With this, he continued to the next door. Reggie stared at him and glanced down at the man smoking. The boyfriend gave a nod to Reggie. Reggie nodded, stepped back into his room, and shut the door.

❊ ❊ ❊

"What we gonna do Bobby?"

Sober, Deborah and Money were having a talk they'd had plenty of times. The conversation was about their current financial situation and what they could do to climb out of the valley.

"Shiid. Grind. Hustle. Only thing we can do," Money said.

"I got a child to raise," she said.

"That girl ain't no damn child. Fo' mo' years and she an adult. Might as well learn what the world is now. Shit ain't sweet out here," he said.

"It ain't got to be sweet, but it's got to be better than this," she said.

"This all she know right now though," he said.

"Is this it? Is this all we got to do out here? Hustling ain't gonna get us outta here Bobby. We ain't no damn gangsters. We're adults. Or at least we're supposed to be," she said.

"Look. I ain't gon' fill your head up with no dreams. Adult or not, this world ain't set up for people like me. I done told you that before. Hell, you a woman. You got mo' chances out here than me," Money said.

"I'm a poor Black woman. That's the same as being a convict. We in the same damn boat. But we gotta figure something out. This shit ain't it man," she said her voice beginning to crack.

Money saw her getting upset and sat beside her on the bed.

"Look baby, no need to get all worked up. Shit ain't perfect, but we making it. We ain't on the street," he said putting his hand on her shoulder.

"Might as well be!" She burst out, throwing his hand off of her.

"Calm down Deb. We gonna make it. Opportunity gon' come," Money said.

Deborah turned and rolled her eyes. She wiped the tears away that had slid down her cheek.

"Listen," he said grabbing her face and turning it towards him. "I got us. I know it don't look like it now, but we gonna get out of here. Keep doing what you doing down at that job and I'll do what I gotta do. Just like I been doing," he said.

She'd heard this before. One too many times. She wanted to believe him, but she knew better. Some men could make things happen. Some wanted to, but for whatever reason, life would never turn in their favor. The man she'd currently latched on to, Money, was the latter. She was in love with the albatross currently around her neck.

"What time you go to work?" He asked.

She looked down at her watch, "In about an hour," she said.

"Take a nap. I'm gonna go out here and see about making some moves," he said.

"What you gonna do?" She asked.

"Let me handle the streets. You just worry about having a good day today."

Money kissed her forehead, stood up, and left.

Deborah watched him leave. She wasn't tired and wouldn't be taking a nap. She saw a cockroach crawl out of a crack by the top hinge on the door. It ran down to the carpet and disappeared under the dresser. She shuddered and looked back at the door.

CHAPTER 24

"You like getting your ass beat by Missy don't you?"

Breanna, working with one of her regulars was performing a frequent client request. Race Play. White men loved the shit and they paid handsomely for her to engage their fetish. She never turned it down because the money was just too good. White man wanted his ass beat by a Black woman? Sure. Why the hell not?

"Answer me White Boy!" She shouted at him.

Breanna cracked him with her cat o' nine tails. He winced.

"Yes, Missy," tonight's Damon said in a combination of excitement and pain.

Truthfully, she took pleasure in this part of the job. Save having to call herself a "Black bitch", beating old White men gave her a sense of satisfaction. She was in full control at that moment and they were at her mercy.

"Squeal!" she shouted as she cracked him with her cat.

He gave his best squeal. Breanna was not satisfied. She made him howl with the next lash.

Reggie had left a note on Breanna's door about taking her out so the two were locked up on this Saturday afternoon. Riding the train, Breanna stared out of the window.

He watched her. Reggie, not usually the romantic, liked spending time with Breanna. Especially away from the motel.

They grabbed Polish sausages from a street vendor for lunch. Both all the way (onions, peppers, and a special sauce they kept secret). They sat on a bench and ate. Traffic moved in a steady flow. City dwellers understood traffic was never light but it calmed down at certain points during the day.

"It's such a beautiful day," Breanna said between bites.

"Yeah. Glad I could spend some time with you outside of the hood," Reggie said laughing. "You be disappearing. I'm surprised you had time."

"Baby I'll always make time for you," she said.

Reggie could see the sincerity in her eyes. He took a bite of his hot dog.

"Yeah, I hear you," he said with his mouth full.

"What you got planned for us today Mr. Man?" Breanna asked.

Reggie thought for a second.

"Planned? In the city?" He laughed. "My plans are seeing what unfolds, to be honest. But, there is a comedy show tonight at 7. You tryna go?"

"Oh. My. God. YES! I've never been to a live show," she said.

"Aight, it's settled then. But, until then, we can see what else is around and relax."

Reggie finished up his Polish, wiped his mouth, and tossed his napkin in the trash. Breanna did the same and stood up after.

"You spoiling me ya know," she said.

"Not really," Reggie said.

"You are," she said and nudged him with her hips.

They kissed and headed down the sidewalk.

❄ ❄ ❄

When they got back to the motel there were cops, detectives, an ambulance, and caution tape placed around four cones surrounding the taco truck. Reggie hoped they weren't there for the Mexican lady that ran the truck. He spotted a cop standing off to the side by himself and approached.

"What happened?" Reggie asked.

The cop, not making eye contact, spoke.

"One of the Mexicans was shot and killed while ordering his food," he said.

Breanna was stunned.

"You haven't seen any suspicious people lurking around, have you? More suspicious than normal in a place like this I mean," the police officer clarified.

They both shook their heads "No".

The cop looked from Reggie to Breanna.

"Looks like a robbery. That's the downside to these food trucks. The people mostly pay in cash and you never know who's watching. Especially at night. They got them new apps, but someone here, not speaking much English, wouldn't bother with them. Thief probably only made off with a few dollars," he said.

"Damn," Reggie said.

Scanning the area, Reggie saw Money in his peripheral. He sat resting on his bike across the street at Smiley's. He observed the scene and seemed to be staring directly at Reggie. They didn't physically acknowledge one another, just stared. Reggie broke the eye contact and pulled Breanna away to his room.

Reggie walked by the taco truck the following morning. The metal blinds on the truck were pulled down. It reminded Reggie of an abandoned house. Although he heard traffic pass, momentarily, no one was outside. He examined the menu. In the window, the overall grade was on display. 92.5 was the number and B was the grade. For what amounted to an outdoor eatery, that grade was high enough.

"Morning, big bro."

Money. His voice interrupted Reggie's train of thought. He'd crept up on his bike and was now behind Reggie.

"What's up," Reggie said as he turned to face Money.

"Shit, I can't call it," Money said. "I seen you over here last night. What the fuck they say happened?"

"Somebody murdered one of the Mexicans," Reggie said.

"Damn. They know who did it?" Money asked.

Reggie stared at Money after his question but eventually broke eye contact.

"Nah. Not that I know of," Reggie said, looking at the taco stand.

"Niggas is foul out here, bro," Money said.

"Yeah," Reggie said dryly.

Truth be told, Reggie had had an inkling that Money had something to do with the murder. After seeing him sitting on his bike the night before with that thousand-yard stare and him popping up this morning, his feeling had only grown stronger. There was nothing he could or would do to prove it, but his gut feeling said Money had robbed and murdered the Mexican man. But, as these things go, he decided to mind his own business. Death was as prominent as these taco trucks on this side of town.

There Is No Sin Without You.

The phrase flashed in his mind again.

"Shit crazy out here, man," Reggie said, not wanting to speak with Money any longer than necessary at this point. "I'm bout to head over to the store."

"Aight, big bro. You stay safe out here," Money said and walked his bike backward. He turned and rode to the opposite side of the building. Towards his room.

Reggie walked to the edge of the driveway leading to the motel. He made a right and headed up the sidewalk. He decided to go to the gas station further up the street instead of Smiley's.

❄ ❄ ❄

It was a solo day for Reggie and it had been an especially exhausting one. The added comfort of working in cold weather brought no relief as he'd cleaned three two-story houses before arriving at what would be the last house on his route. The rooms that needed to be cleaned in all of the houses were upstairs so he had to lug the vacuum hose, steam line, and cleaning products upstairs each time. With this, he had to tie the hoses at the top of the steps to prevent them from sliding back down as he cleaned. On days that he was lazy and didn't tie them, he had to continuously pull the hoses back up the stairs because of how slowly yet consistently they'd slide down the steps and end up at the bottom. A potential tripping hazard for himself and the customers. He missed Dustin pulling the hoses out of the room for him as he had to stop constantly to throw more and more hose out of the room as he cleaned his way out.

His shirt was drenched after the first house and when he stepped outside to grab spot cleaner from the van or to adjust the pressure for the vacuum hose, the combination of his damp shirt and the cold air made his teeth rattle. The fresh air was welcome initially, but it made his body stiffen. He shook off the feeling each time before he began cleaning again.

The last house was just a single room that needed to be cleaned. A hallway to be precise. A moving company had been contacted by the husband to assist the small family of three in moving old furniture out of the home and had tracked mud onto the carpet.

Reggie need not bother selling any more services as the moving company was fronting the bill and the homeowners would need to schedule a separate cleaning to make adjustments on what needed to be cleaned.

This job seemed straightforward. The drive between the third and fourth house (the house he was now parked in front of) had been 40 minutes. The intensity of the heat in the van and the meshlike material the company shirts were made from helped to dry him off between jobs. At least, at this point, he was mostly dry.

Finished reading the notes for the job, Reggie engaged the parking brake, grabbed the tablet, and climbed out of the van.

His boxers, damp from his heavy sweating, stuck to his thighs. He adjusted them to loosen their grip as they had begun riding up and headed to the front door.

He was greeted immediately as Daniel, the owner of the house, opened the door and stepped out onto the porch.

"Evening," Daniel said.

"How's it going?" Reggie said.

"Depends on if you can get this dirt out of my carpet," Daniel said.

Reggie chuckled.

"I'll see what I can do," Reggie said.

Daniel looked to be in his late thirties. His hair was buzzed short to make his balding less noticeable. Reggie could see Daniel's gray eyes behind the black-framed glasses he wore.

"Wanna show me where the damage was done?" Reggie asked.

"Sure," Daniel replied.

To Reggie's surprise, Daniel shut the door and started leading him down the steps.

"Follow me. The entrance is on the side of the house," Daniel said noticing the look of confusion on Reggie's face.

"Gotcha," Reggie said.

Daniel led Reggie to the side of the house to a set of steps that led down to the basement. This caught Reggie by surprise as it hadn't been mentioned that the hallway was in the basement. He followed Daniel down the steps.

"It's just through this door," Daniel said.

270

In addition to the hallway, the movers had also tracked mud into the main room in the basement and the steps leading up to the door to the house. All carpeted. Once he'd squared away what he was cleaning, he sent pictures back to Chris to let him know of the mix-up in the amount of cleaning that needed to be done. Chris acknowledged the mistake and told Reggie to proceed with cleaning as normal. He made sure to bill the movers the correct price along with showing them the pictures of the damaged areas.

Reggie moved the van to the side of the house so as not to drag the hoses further than necessary. Knowing this was the last house gave him added motivation to finish the job quickly.

The basement was a man cave. There was a flat-screen television mounted on the wall. 55" he guessed. Two gaming systems (an XBOX and a Playstation). A new couch, plastic still intact, was pushed into the corner along with a gaming chair and other necessities to outfit Daniel's personal space.

The mud was heavier in some spots and had dried after having sat for two days. The thought of stealing anything had not entered Reggie's mind. He initially believed he might give it a go before the day began, but after the first house, he abandoned the idea. This had been a normal cleaning day. So normal that Reggie laughed at the thought that he'd all but forgotten what it felt like to earn his daily bread the old-fashioned way.

Besides, looking around, there wasn't anything to steal in Daniel's basement.

Who kept jewelry in the basement anyway? Reggie thought to himself.

Stealing one of the gaming systems was out of the question. They were the newer systems, so they'd fetch a couple hundred at the pawnshop (and even more if he sold them online), but he'd be caught before the end of the day. At the very least, he'd be caught once the carpet dried and Daniel came down to situate everything where he wanted it.

It was Wednesday. Dustin would be back tomorrow and for the remainder of the week so he could make up for today.

He got the van set up, drug the hoses down to the basement, and started cleaning.

❅ ❅ ❅

Reggie sat at the desk in the motel sipping his beer. He had already eaten the Chinese food he'd ordered on his way home. House rice and wings. Usually, he tried to save some, but on this night, exhausted, he ate everything. Leaving only chicken bones and a few grains of rice in the styrofoam box most Chinese restaurants placed their to-go orders in.

He was tired but also prideful in the work he'd put in. There was something human about taking pride in working hard. He wasn't going to be doing manual labor for the rest of his life, but the feeling of working with his hands gave him a sense of pride that he never expressed, but felt innately at times.

Having showered and fed what felt like a feast to his tired body, he sipped his beer and stared at the wall in front of him. It was chipped in spots, had scratches, and was also discolored. Probably from years of smoke from previous occupants.

He sipped and thought. Thought about finally getting out of this shit stain of a motel. Thought about life on the other side. The side where people weren't looking over their shoulders, where gunshots were replaced with the sounds of lawnmowers, where neighbors weren't merely potential scam victims but human beings.

Deep down he did feel remorse for robbing people of their possessions. He gulped his beer at the thought.

He wouldn't stop. This was where his life was at. Where America was. And he'd make no qualms about getting his piece of the pie.

CHAPTER 25

Reggie purchased a .38 Special from *Stick-Up Pawn Shop* once he'd saved up enough money.

The selection wasn't that large, but he wasn't looking for anything out of the ordinary.

He'd only shot a BB gun before, but he'd learn to shoot quickly if he had to. There was a shooting range he could take his gun to as well. He figured he may need it for one of the addicts who hung around the motel before needing it on a job, but owning it gave him peace of mind.

He paid cash for the .38 at the register. The chubby young Mexican employee rang him up. He wasn't sure what questions he'd expected to be asked but just figured a line of questioning was necessary to make sure they didn't sell to one of the gun-happy madcaps that were everywhere in the country now.

The questions never came though. He'd only needed to pass a background check. Didn't even need a permit. He bought the gun, a box of ammo and tucked both into a bookbag. Couldn't risk anyone on the bus seeing a weapon. People became nervous when they realized the threat of death was around. Or they acted accordingly.

The young Mexican handed him his items and Reggie left the shop.

❄ ❄ ❄

They heard the dog barking on the other side of the door.

Reggie and Dustin waited for the homeowner to answer.

The house was nice and they figured they'd get their hands on a few items but hearing the dog had changed Reggie's mind.

"It's a go if they put the dog up," Reggie said.

"It's a go either way," Dustin said.

They'd been careful up to this point. Not being caught had made Dustin bold as time went on. Which would only lead to him being careless if Reggie didn't grab the reigns.

"We're not doing shit if that dog is as big as it sounds and they don't at least lock him in a room," Reggie said.

He looked at Dustin who didn't respond.

"Hey, guys!"

A brunette thirty-something White female homeowner opened the door. She wore gray sweat pants and a white tank top.

"Hi," they said in unison.

The black Labrador moseyed around her legs and stood next to her at the door; tail wagging staring at both Reggie and Dustin.

Reggie noticed that one of its eyes was brown and the other blue. It reminded him of a dog from his neighborhood. Jaws was the name of the massive pitbull with one brown eye and one blue eye. Jaws was a mean dog and his owner had fought him with other dogs in the neighborhood. When he decided he didn't want the dog anymore, he tied its mouth shut with duck tape and beat it to death with a baseball bat. The kids in the neighborhood didn't find out what happened to Jaws until months after. There was outrage, but those were years when people minded their own business. For better or for worse.

"Could you two wait here while I put him up?" She asked looking at both men.

"Sure," Reggie said.

"Thanks. I'll just be a minute. He gets worked up around strangers. Not in a bad way, just gets too excited," she said and pulled the dog away by the collar and shut the door.

"Like I said, it's go time," Dustin said.

"I hear you," Reggie said. "Just stay focused and make sure-"

The door opened cutting Reggie off.

"Y'all can come in now," she said pulling the front door all the way open to invite the two men inside.

Reggie gave Dustin one last look and the two stepped inside.

"I'm Dorothy by the way, but call me Dot, please. I was named after my grandmother, but I've never grown into that name. Loved that woman though," Dot said.

Reggie guessed her age to be in the late twenties. She wore those spandex jogging pants that all the ladies were wearing. Hers were gray. She wore a plain pink sweatshirt and had her hair tied in a ponytail. She may grow into Dorothy in the next 20-30 years, but for now, Dot was fitting.

"I'm Reggie," he said.

"Dustin," Dustin said looking around the living room.

Reggie noticed there were no traces of a man. Everything about the home was feminine. *She's single* he thought to himself.

His train of thought was stopped by the dog barking in an upstairs bedroom.

He'll be out of the way," Dot said.

"How old is he?" Reggie asked.

"He's about to be a year old soon. Got him when I first moved in. He's my protector," she said.

"I can tell he don't play when it comes to you," Reggie said.

Dot laughed. "He's all bark for now."

On cue, Shemar barked again from upstairs.

"See what I mean?" Dot said laughing.

"I definitely do. Wanna show us which rooms we'll be cleaning?" Reggie asked.

"Sure. It's the living room, the stairs, and upstairs hallway, my bedroom, and the guest room across from the bathroom down here. There aren't any real problem areas besides a spot next to the nightstand in my bedroom. He's peed there a few times the past couple of weeks," Dot said.

"Urine stains may or may not come out. It tends to get into the carpet padding. Specially if that's his favorite spot. One thing I do recommend is that you get deodorizer. The hot steam bath from our equipment is gonna wake that smell up and perfume the room with it," Reggie said.

"I see. Okay. How much is the deodorizer?"

"$20," Reggie said.

"Add it," Dot said with no hesitation.

Dustin exited the home while Dot signed the slip and fall notice.

"She's hot as fuck," Dustin said as he unraveled the vacuum hose from the back of the van.

"Yeah, she's nice," Reggie said.

"Hot," Dustin emphasized.

"You want to skip this one?" Reggie asked. Dustin stopped unraveling.

"We're not skipping anything," he said firmly. "We're not thieves with hearts of gold. We're just two poor working men doing what we gotta do to keep our heads above water. I'm not doing some privileged White chick able to afford a house on a single salary no favors. That doesn't change the fact that I think she's gorgeous," Dustin said.

Reggie didn't say it aloud, but he silently agreed.

"Well, keep your eyes open when we get in the bedroom. Won't be able to grab anything downstairs," Reggie said.

Dustin nodded and continued unraveling the hose.

❄ ❄ ❄

As was the custom, they began cleaning in the furthest room. The master bedroom. Shemar was locked in a separate room down the hallway. He'd barked with all the strength in his lungs as they drug the hoses past the room he was locked in. Dot yelled for him to quiet down. Hearing her voice had quieted him momentarily, but he was soon barking again.

There were pictures of Dot with her family on her dresser. Reggie stopped to look at a picture of an older woman. She wore a blue dress with a slit down the middle that led to her bust line. Around her neck was a pearl necklace. She had a closed-mouth smile and was looking off to the right of the camera.

279

Reggie assumed this to be the Dorothy from which Dot had gotten her namesake.

He looked around the room. There were no valuables in sight. He looked back at the picture of Dorothy and wondered whether Dot had received the pearls from the picture. Maybe they had been gifted to her in her grandmother's will. But where would she keep such an heirloom he thought to himself. He saw no jewelry box.

He walked next to the nightstand. The carpet was light brown, but the stain Dot mentioned stood out to him immediately. He'd seen enough animal piss since working at Fair Zone to recognize all kinds of stains that he may have overlooked before. He sprayed a solution over the spot to help loosen the fibers.

He heard Shemar start up again and knew Dustin was approaching.

Dustin gave him a look when he entered the room that said *You see anything good?*

Reggie shook his head *no*.

He pointed at the picture of Dorothy on the dresser.

Dustin walked over and picked it up.

Reggie motioned about the pearl necklace. Dustin quickly glanced around the room but saw exactly what Reggie saw. Nothing.

Reggie attached the wand to the vacuum hose and began cleaning.

Dustin slid the nightstand out of the way so Reggie could clean the entire area. The top drawer slid open as he did so. He glanced inside and saw the necklace.

His eyes lit up.

He grabbed it and tapped Reggie on the shoulder. Reggie looked back at Dustin and then down at the necklace.

"Where was it?" He said keeping his voice just above the suction noise from the vacuum.

"In the nightstand," Dustin said.

"Keep it in your pocket," Reggie said.

Dustin slid the necklace into his pocket.

"Aight, let's knock this job out and get out of here," Reggie said.

Reggie was halfway finished cleaning the bedroom when Shemar trotted in.

Both he and Dustin froze.

She must lock him in that room enough that he's learned how to get out Reggie thought to himself.

Shemar stood in front of Dustin growling.

"Oh shit," Reggie said aloud. "Put it back before Dot comes up here. That dog knows. He'll sniff it off you when she walks in."

Dustin moved his hand towards his pocket, but Shemar barked when he did snapping Dustin back into formation.

Reggie had to think quickly. He misted Shemar with the wand. A bit of water got into the dog's eyes breaking his stand-off with Dustin. He pushed the wand in the dog's direction.

"Shemar!" Dot called from downstairs.

"Shit!" Dustin said.

Reggie misted the dog once more.

"Put it back," Reggie said motioning for Dustin to return the necklace to the nightstand.

He backed the dog out of the room and saw Dot coming up the stairs. Her pace quickened to a light jog once she saw that Shemar had gotten out of the room. She grabbed his collar. He began barking at Reggie. She peaked into the bedroom. Dustin, finished putting the necklace back, was standing by the door.

"I'm sorry," she said. "I forgot he knows how to get out.

She noticed the nightstand had been moved.

"Careful with that stand," she said without mentioning more. Reggie looked back at Dustin and then at the stand.

"We got you," he said.

"I'll put him out back," she said and tugged the barking dog down the stairs.

"Let's take it," Dustin said.

"You done lost your mind. She knows we've at least touched the nightstand and with the dog going crazy like that, that's the first thing she's gonna check when we leave. This mission is officially aborted," Reggie said.

Dustin thought about it. He seemed to come to the same conclusion.

"Stupid mutt. Just barked us out of a big payday," he said.

The two were a little shaken by the encounter but managed to gather themselves and finish the job. When Dustin grabbed the chip bucket from the hallway, he noticed Shemar had pissed in it.

The remainder of the workday was tame. The excitement (more unnerving than exciting of course) at Dot's had been the climax. No other homeowner or apartment dweller had a pet. And that was for the best Reggie rationalized as he sat on the edge of his bed back at Competitive Inn.

They hadn't even swiped anything from the remaining cleaning jobs. Nothing worth stealing they'd reasoned after each job.

Silently though, they were both a little too shaken from how close they'd been to getting caught and possibly mauled by a one-year-old Labrador for their troubles.

Maybe having this scare early in the operation was good. Before they got too cocky and that feeling of being untouchable set in. Humble precision was better than cocky carelessness.

Dustin needed to be humbled. Hopefully, today emphasized just what it was they were doing and how high the stakes were. By the look on his face and his reluctance to pocket any valuables the remainder of the day, whether he'd admit it or not, reality had sunk in.

Today was less of a setback and more so a learning experience.

❄ ❄ ❄

Days passed and both men had put the incident behind them.

Reggie decided to head to Kannapolis early the next morning with today's batch of jewelry. They had gotten two diamond necklaces, a pair of earrings, and a bracelet on the day.

He stole the earrings. Dustin stole everything else. Reggie needed to stick to the cleaning schedule so as not to linger longer than necessary in any of the houses. Especially after they swiped something. Dustin had time to look around while keeping tabs on the customer's whereabouts in the home.

❄ ❄ ❄

It wasn't late, but outside was black. They'd finished up early so Reggie had been back at the motel for several hours. He'd gotten some Chinese food on his way back and was watching television when they knocked on the door.

The knock wasn't pronounced. It was either Breanna or another of Money's customers Reggie figured. Full from the Chinese food and halfway asleep, Reggie turned on the lights in the room and answered the door.

The two officers from the sex offender accosting stared at him. Reggie hadn't drunk beer nor smoked so he was instantly alert.

Fuck he thought to himself. *Someone fucking told.*

"How you doing Mr. Skinter," the lead officer who remembered Reggie from the previous encounter asked.

Reggie was taken aback by them calling him by name but remembered he'd given the officer his identification the last time.

"What's this about?" Reggie asked ignoring the officer's greeting.

"We're asking the questions tonight Mr. Skinter," the lead officer said.

They stared at one another in silent understanding before the officer continued.

"Is there someone in there with you?" He asked.

"No," Reggie said.

Reggie looked in the room and saw he'd forgotten to put away the bracelet from the job earlier in the day. His heart sank.

The officer saw the look on his face change and looked past him into the room. He spotted the expensive bracelet sitting on the only dresser in the room. It lay in plain sight next to the television.

"What's that?" He asked.

285

Reggie's speech failed him for a moment.

"A gift," he said managing to keep his voice from cracking.

"For?" The officer prodded.

"Why is that any of your business," he said.

His confidence was beginning to return. Besides, what business was it of theirs what he had in his room. They'd need to announce their intentions. He wasn't gonna give himself up unnecessarily.

"Just asking. Not too many people have expensive jewelry on this side of town. Not real jewelry anyway. From here, that looks pretty expensive," the officer said.

"It's not real," Reggie said.

"Mind if I have a look at it?" The officer asked with a demanding tone.

Reggie thought about saying no, but if these pigs were here for nothing, that would only prolong this unwanted interaction. And possibly make him more of a target for these meetings than he already was. He was starting to suspect that they wanted to bust him for drugs. There were several dealers that came and went into the motel. They just didn't know who was who.

He grabbed the bracelet from in front of the television and handed it to the officer. He took a long look at it. Even held it up in a bit of awe to his partner whose eyes shifted from the bracelet back to Reggie.

"You sure this is fake Mr. Skinter?"

"It was sold to me for a fake price if that makes sense," Reggie said.

"It doesn't," the lead responded flatly.

"I clean carpets officer. I couldn't afford that piece of jewelry if it was real," he kept a straight face and locked eyes with the officer.

Even if the officer was able to sniff a lie, he couldn't prove anything. If they had come knocking because they'd caught wind from a customer, the conversation would've ended already. If he could stay calm, he was confident he could get out of this jam.

The officer stared at the bracelet and then at his partner. After some time, he looked back to Reggie.

"Fair enough. Looks damn real though, I wouldn't tell whoever you're gifting it to that you paid less than top-shelf price," the officer said.

Reggie didn't respond. The officer handed him back the bracelet.

"Sorry to keep dropping in on you like this," the officer said. "You seen any activity around here lately?"

"Activity? What kind of activity?" Reggie asked knowing exactly what they meant.

"Drugs," the officer said.

"No," Reggie said.

"You sure? There are a lot of dealers in the area. You seem like a decent man. If you have to stay at this place, no need to defend the monsters that hang around seedy shitholes like this," the officer said.

You're one of those monsters Reggie thought to himself.

"I don't speak to anybody here and I'm at work during the day. Couldn't tell you the daily happenings if I wanted to. I'm just trying to get by like everyone else in this place," Reggie said.

There was silence. The officer realized he wouldn't be getting any more information from Reggie.

"Well, you have a good night. Hopefully, we won't run into you again," the officer said with something extra in his voice.

The tone upset Reggie.

"Hope not," he said.

Both officers nodded at Reggie and headed down the steps to their squad car. Reggie waited in the doorway for a bit. Just to make sure they left. They pulled off and he shut the door.

He put the bracelet with the rest of the jewelry; inside the nightstand beside the bed. He need not be careless with how he handled things. They hadn't been there about the jewelry, but if they had, he'd be sitting in the back of their squad car headed to the station right now.

With everything else going on in the area and the city in general, he had two pigs that had taken a liking to him. He wouldn't be giving them anything to further their, as of yet, unfounded suspicions. He was proud of himself for how he handled the situation, but the goal was to be under the radar. The least attention the better.

Another one and a half months and it'd be over. He'd have enough to leave this motel, Fair Zone, Money, and the nosy cops that hung around seedy shitholes like this behind.

He hadn't spoken to Breanna in awhile and now wondered if she was in her room. He left to find out.

CHAPTER 26

Reggie sat on the bed counting his portion of the money after the split with Dustin. He'd been to countless pawn shops the past few weeks, but it was the best way to keep from causing raised eyebrows at the amount of stuff he'd been bringing in to sell. He counted $4500 in total in the stack he held in his hand.

Truthfully, he knew it wasn't much, but it felt good to have. If only because he knew he'd be able to skip town if a job were to go awry.

Dustin's attitude toward his girlfriend's pregnancy had changed for the better. He beamed when he told Reggie that they were expecting a girl. Though he didn't cry while he was talking, Reggie did see tears well up a few times as Dustin spoke about how much things had turned around the last couple of months.

I wouldn't mind if this money was permanent Dustin had said as they spoke. Reggie noticed how sad Dustin looked as reality sunk in. The slow season wouldn't last forever and they wouldn't need to continue using Fair Zone's customers to supplement their paychecks. But they had made significantly more during this time than they would have made otherwise.

The .38 sat next to him on the bed. It'd been a while since one of Money's customers had knocked on the door. And he hadn't had anyone trying to break in either.

Reggie thumbed through the money once more.

"Stop!"

The wall rattled. Reggie, startled, sat upright.

There was a thud. Reggie could tell Money had shoved Deborah into the wall.

Reggie heard what was probably the three of them tussling. Slaps and punches sounded off from the room.

There was another thud. This time Money had been shoved into the wall.

"You better get her before I kill that little girl!" Money yelled.

"Get out!" Deborah screamed.

"I ain't going nowhere. I pay my half just like you. If y'all wanna leave, bye!" Money said.

Reggie put his ear to the wall to listen. He wasn't normally interested, but it had been a while since they'd

291

had a physical fight. With all the banging on the wall, they'd forced him into the situation.

"You a sorry mutha-fucka Bobby. I hope they kill your stupid ass out there," Deborah said.

"Ain't nobody gon' do a mutha-fuckin' thang to me. I run these streets. I'm Money. These niggas need me out here," Money said.

"Ain't never got no fucking money, but they need you. You as dumb as those crackheads," Deborah said.

"But you still wit my dumbass so what that make you?" Money asked.

"Let's just leave ma. This nigga ain't bout shit. I can get a job. Fuck him!" Victoria yelled.

"Then leave. Ain't nobody holding y'all hostage. The door's right there," Money said.

Reggie waited to hear the door open but it never did. From what Reggie could make of these monthly fights, the relationship had long soured, but neither would leave. Not now at least. Struggling with a partner was easier. They'd stick it out until one killed the other.

Their voices softened eventually and Reggie turned on the television.

❄ ❄ ❄

"I went by your room the other night."

Reggie and Breanna were sitting on a bench at the park. Both held cups of cappuccino they'd purchased at a gas station before coming.

"What time?" She asked.

"Night obviously," Reggie laughed.

"Right," she laughed. "I got in late most of the week. I thought about stopping by, but I wanted you to get your rest for work," Breanna said.

"Ah, you coulda knocked. I can always sleep," he said.

"You missed me, huh?" She asked playfully.

"You cool," he said looking away.

There weren't many people at the park. A few joggers in windbreakers ran laps around the pond and a woman watched her two children play on the equipment.

"Uh-huh," Breanna said. "I talked to that Indian man the other day."

"What Indian man?" Reggie asked.

"The one that works at the motel. The young one," she said.

"Isaac. I've talked to him a few times. He's pretty cool. Doesn't bother you as long as you pay your bill on time. Did something happen?" he asked and took a sip from his cup.

"No, nothing happened. He caught me while I was leaving. He was waiting for an ambulance to come," Breanna said.

"Ambulance? Why was he waiting for the meat wagon?" He asked.

"He said an older woman died in her room. It was check-out time and he went to see if she was gone or in the process of leaving. Said he knocked and opened

293

the door with his key when he didn't hear anything. It looked like she was asleep. That's how he described it. He left and came back 15 minutes later to see if she'd woken up or to wake her up. She was still in the same position when he walked in the room. He nudged her and she didn't move. Dead," Breanna said.

"So the body was still in the room while y'all were outside talking," Reggie asked.

She nodded.

"Yep. I didn't peak inside the room or anything. He said she'd only been there for three days. Not dead. She'd been staying at the motel for three days. She went by the lobby the night before for toilet paper so he did see her alive recently," she said.

"Damn," Reggie said.

"He said she had no family. Sixty-two years old and she died alone in that motel. *All we can do is pray for these people*," Breanna said.

"What do you mean?"

"That's what Isaac said. *All we can do is pray for these people*," she repeated.

"Yeah, I-," Reggie started, but was quickly interrupted.

"We're those people. Living in the motel. I don't know really. It just sounded like he felt sorry for the people that stay there. But in a judgy way," she said.

"Well, whatever they *feel*, they make money off of the situation either way. So, they don't feel bad enough that they'd want people not to stay there. They provide a cheap place to die and one hand washes the other," Reggie said.

"That's probably oversimplifying, but that's the gist of it from what I could make of what he was trying to say. The ambulance pulled up when I got down the steps," Breanna said.

Reggie didn't say anything. It had been some time since they'd gotten a chance to sit down together and he didn't want to sully the time with such a morbid topic.

"What you doing when the summertime comes around?" He asked.

Breanna wasn't even sure she'd still be at Competitive when the summer came around. Saving money aside, living around so much destruction was causing her patience to run thin. Presently, she looked over at Reggie who was ogling her with the look she'd seen from so many of her Damon's.

"I haven't made any plans. Why do you wanna know?" Breanna asked.

"Thinking about getting away from Competitive around that time. For good," Reggie said.

"Where you going?" She asked.

He didn't know. But he'd have enough money by then to stay somewhere nicer than the disease-ridden motel the both of them were currently staying.

"I still got a little time to figure that out," Reggie said.

She kissed him.

"If you're asking me to come with you.. Maybe. But you don't even know where you're going right now," Breanna said.

"Don't be concerned with the details. I wouldn't ask the question if I couldn't afford you," he said.

"I like the energy. Keep me posted on what you decide and we'll see what happens," she said.

He didn't like her response, but he could tell it was an honest one. There was no need to pressure her into making a decision.

"I guess I'll take that," Reggie said.

"You don't have a choice," she smirked and slid closer.

He put his arm around her and they both sipped their cappuccinos and observed the light activity around the park.

CHAPTER 27

Chris had scheduled a night job. A rarity, but he'd said the customer paid well so he didn't mind making the accommodations. He was only available after hours so he needed to be assigned a specific day and time to make sure he received regular cleanings.

Reggie didn't usually volunteer for cleaning jobs after hours, but once he'd learned the guy was wealthy, he jumped at the opportunity. It didn't take much to convince Dustin. He only needed to get permission from his boss (cause women were naturally suspicious when men were out late) and he was set for the job.

Reggie tucked his bookbag behind the driver's seat in his van before they left Fair Zone. No one else was at the shop. Chris had told them what they'd needed to know for the job earlier in the day. The job was a standard cleaning. He said there were a lot of floors to clean, but the owner was cool. He'd also told Reggie that his card was on file and that he didn't have to worry about collecting payment when they were done. They could just pack up and leave.

He still hadn't shot the gun yet, but he felt good knowing it was close.

❊ ❊ ❊

It was after eight when they pulled into the neighborhood. Dark except for the moonlight and lamp post that lined the streets, Reggie could still make out the immense size of the house. He pulled the van around the circular driveway and parked in front.

Reggie checked the notes in his tablet

Dustin waited silently in the passenger seat.

The customer's name was George Thomas. They cleaned his carpets for the past couple of years from what Reggie read in the notes. All night jobs. The night jobs, as few as there were, were posted on a separate board in the Route Room. He never had a reason to check it so he stayed away so he didn't give the managers the impression that he cared to take a job when one was posted.

"Alright. This is our first night job. The house is going to be darker than normal so we gotta keep things tight. Make sure you keep an eye out for any small things we can take easy while we're doing the walkthrough," Reggie said.

"Cool. I know what to do," Dustin said. "I'm thinking tonight might be the jackpot. How you feel?"

Reggie stared out the windshield at the house. They'd gotten lucky up until now. But nothing had been the jackpot that Dustin was referring to. He didn't know. But just like he needed to scratch the spots to match the winning number, they'd need to go inside to see if this was the jackpot.

"Maybe. He for sure has some bread. We'll see what's what once we get inside," Reggie said.

They saw a light on the porch turn on. George opened the door and stepped outside a moment later. He waved at the van.

"You ready?" Reggie said.

Dustin nodded and they both got out.

❊ ❊ ❊

George lived alone.

After the walkthrough, he chatted with Reggie and Dustin for a bit and went to his study. He had other work to attend to and trusted that the two men could find their way around the house.

Reggie and Dustin, finished setting up the van and dragging the hoses inside, got started cleaning upstairs.

A few watches lay across the dresser in the master bedroom. They varied in the brand and watch type, but they were all luxury watches.

The few paintings he had in his bedroom looked expensive. Reggie wasn't an artist and didn't recognize the painters, but they looked like work from the Romanticism era.

Dustin stood at the door staring at Reggie. He wanted to look around but decided not to. He feared he might run into George on accident. The night made the rest of the house seem quieter than it probably was. The house was also large enough that if he got turned around in the dark, he could find himself having to explain what he was doing.

George had asked that Reggie clean the carpet in the walk-in closet that was connected to the master bathroom.

Reggie opened the door that led to the closet and drug the hose inside.

Dustin walked into the room and watched him clean. There were suits, casual clothes, and shoes. Nothing stood out. He brushed his hand across the suits. Not his style dress-wise, but they were nice.

"Shut that door so I can clean behind it," Reggie shouted at Dustin over the sound of the vacuum hose.

Dustin backed out of the room and shut the door.

Reggie opened the door, eyes wide as he stared at Dustin. He motioned for Dustin to come back inside.

Dustin walked in, looked behind the door, and saw a safe sitting on the floor.

"What you think he got in there?" Reggie asked.

"I'm guessing some money. Maybe jewelry. There could be anything in there really," Dustin said.

"You think he got shit like that in a safe on the floor?"

"On the floor in his closet. Nobody's coming up here. That safe behind the picture shit is for the movies," Dustin said.

Reggie thought about what Dustin said. It made sense. And the neighborhood looked nice enough that paranoia probably wasn't the norm. But now, the fact that it was *for the movies* worked in their favor.

"You might be right. It's a digital lock," he said bending down to pull the handle. "I don't think we'll be able to-"

The door of the safe opened with minimal effort. It hadn't been locked. Or the lock was broken. Reggie wasn't an expert. George had probably not gotten around to replacing it and hadn't thought to move it before having the crew over.

"Oh shit," Dustin said. "It ain't locked."

Reggie motioned for Dustin to bring his voice down.

"Relax," Reggie said.

He opened the safe. There was $40,000 in cash on the small shelf.

More money than either of them had ever seen at one time.

They both looked at each other at the same time.

"We gotta take all of it," Dustin said.

"We can't," Reggie said.

Dustin's face showed how much he agonized hearing him say this.

"Why can't we? He won't know til' whenever. By that time, it won't even matter. I say we take it all. We gotta take it all Reg," Dustin said almost pleading with him.

Reggie looked down at the money in the safe.

"How about we take half. If he sees an empty safe we're done. At least he may think twice if we leave some of the money. If somebody had taken any of the money, why not take it all, right? He might think he took some as spending money or something," Reggie said.

Dustin knew he was making sense, but he didn't care. He was looking at $40,000 and couldn't think of a good reason not to take it all. They were already taking chances and everything had gone smoothly so far.

"Alright, let's do that," Dustin said.

Reggie grabbed $20,000 and handed $10,000 to Dustin. They folded the money and slid it into their pockets. Reggie finished cleaning the bedroom afterward.

❀ ❀ ❀

Reggie had made sure the safe was left partially open like he had found it. Cleaning the next couple of rooms seemed to go by in a blur. Reggie could barely focus on the job. The money seemed to be burning in his pocket. Dustin was just as anxious to finish the job and leave the house. Reggie couldn't blame him. This had been the jackpot that he had mentioned.

George hadn't left the study once while they were cleaning. This only made the two men more hurried to finish. They could hear him talking on the phone and typing occasionally, but the rest of the house remained quiet otherwise.

Dustin helped Reggie drag the hoses through the kitchen to a guest room that was located down a hallway near the side entrance to the house.

"Go grab the wand from upstairs," Reggie said.

Dustin paused as he remembered where they'd left the wand.

"Cool. I'll be right back," Dustin said.

Reggie suctioned the vacuum hose to the bedspread to suppress the noise.

He walked back to the door and looked down the hallway. He didn't hear anything. He stepped back into the room, sat on the bed and pulled the $10,000 out of his pocket, and ruffled through the stack of $100 bills.

Maybe he'd finish up the slow season and put in his two weeks at Fair Zone. Dustin could do what he wanted with his cut. He would be a father soon. He imagined the extra money would make his girlfriend happy. If he was smart, he'd be able to figure out a way to invest in a better life for the three of them.

BOOM!

Reggie heard what he knew (from living at Competitive) was a gunshot. But he hadn't brought his .38 in the house and Dustin hadn't mentioned owning a gun of any kind.

He rushed out of the room.

❋ ❋ ❋

"What the fuck were you doing in my closet?" George asked Dustin as he looked down at him.

Dustin tried to speak but couldn't. He had taken a bullet to his chest. From the way he gasped, George could tell the bullet probably hit a lung. As long as it hadn't hit anything major, it might collapse, but Dustin had a good chance of survival. As long as he could get an ambulance.

He walked into his bedroom and came back into the closet with his cellphone in hand. He was dialing 911-

Reggie had never meant for the robberies to get to this point. If Dustin had grabbed the wand and come back downstairs, he'd still be alive. He hadn't heard George leave his study to grab something from his bedroom. George caught him taking the money and threatened to call the police. He brandished a .9mm and pulled the trigger once he saw Dustin make a move towards him.

Reggie, who had heard the commotion, went and grabbed his .38 from the van. He came back upstairs and saw George dialing 911 and Dustin lying on the floor dead or almost there as he bled out on the carpet.

He'd never taken anyone's life before now. It was an odd thing to have to take a man's life as a result of your actions. Even if you felt those actions were forced upon you.

George had taken a headshot from the .38 as soon as Reggie walked through the door. The blood had splattered onto the still wet carpet. Thinking back, he couldn't remember if George's phone hit the floor before his body did or not. *I wonder if Red Wine Remover could get that out?* Reggie thought absently as he looked at all the blood.

"I'm sorry it went down like this man," Reggie said as he looked down at Dustin whose breathing had begun to slow.

Dustin was looking up at Reggie. Reggie could see in his eyes he wanted to say something.

He packed the watches and cash from the safe. Dustin had stopped breathing altogether. He and George lay dead next to one another. Reggie ruffled through Dustin's pockets and found the $10,000.

He left without looking back. Death loomed in the room after.

❋ ❋ ❋

It was dark when Reggie arrived back at the motel. Smoke billowed out of the top of the taco truck. It was still open.

Reggie was hungry and knew he'd grab two tacos before leaving Competitive for good.

The Mexican lady poked her head out of the window, spotted him, and smiled.

Besides the occasional car passing, no one else was in sight.

He went to room 237 first. The curtain for the window was open and the room was dark. A telltale sign of a vacancy.

He went down to the front desk. Isaac had drifted to sleep with his head back and mouth open. The news was on the television.

Reggie pushed the buzzer and he snapped awake; almost falling out of his chair in the process.

Seeing Reggie on the other side of the glass, his face went from aggravated to friendly.

"My friend. What can I do for you?" Isaac asked.

"She checked out?" Reggie asked.

Isaac knew instantly who Reggie was referring to.

"Yes. This morning at 10:30," he said with empathy in his voice.

They stared at one another.

"Figures," Reggie said. "I appreciate you, man."

Isaac smiled and nodded.

"Have a good night my friend," he said.

"You do the same," Reggie said.

The two men weren't close enough to tell him that he was leaving. Nor did he need anyone to be able to give a heads up if and when they came looking for him. Reggie left the office. Isaac waited until he was out of sight and rested back in his chair.

❀ ❀ ❀

Certain women won't be kept. Can't be kept. Sure they'll sit still for a moment. Long enough to pull feelings out

306

that you didn't care to know existed, but they always wrestled themselves away in the end.

Reggie took the money from underneath the mattress and packed everything that he cared to take into his suitcase and guzzled the last Budweiser in the mini-fridge.

He killed a roach on the dresser before tossing the can in the trash. He'd served his last tour in the war against the roaches at Competitive Inn. They'd win eventually, but he'd fought the fight valiantly.

He left the room key on the dresser next to the television.

❊ ❊ ❊

"Two please."

"Onions and cilantro?" She asked.

"And tomatoes on both," Reggie said.

"Ten minutes," the Mexican lady said and turned to throw steak on the grill.

Reggie stood with his suitcase next to him. He heard the sizzle from the grill as the meat began to cook.

The beer had calmed his nerves. He'd all but forgotten about the two bodies that would be discovered at some point in the night. Though it was likely they'd be found in the morning he figured. He thought of Vince and remembered that things like that depended on how important one was. He figured George had been more important than Vince. And Dustin's girlfriend would kick up dust about him not coming home.

He planned on being long gone before then.

He'd call Chris in the morning and make something up about having to leave town. It was unlike him, but that alone wouldn't raise any suspicion. Not at first.

And by the time it did-

"Green sauce?" The Mexican lady asked.

Her voice broke Reggie's train of thought.

"Yes," he said. "Two cups please."

"50 cents," she said.

Reggie nodded in agreement.

He pulled out $100, handed it to her, and waved her off for the change.

"Thank you," she said smiling.

"Great tacos," he said giving her a thumbs up.

Reggie knew how much pride she took in her tacos from the look on her face.

He nodded in appreciation, grabbed his bag, and left. He'd never see her again.

Reggie had enough to get out of Mecklenburg County. Starting over was neither hard nor a bad thing. He could afford an apartment with the money. He'd find a job wherever he ended up. He didn't believe in karma, but on the off chance it caught up to him, he planned to have as much saved as he could. Maybe she'd take a bribe.

Made in the USA
Monee, IL
24 June 2022

98567435R00182